I could feel something stirring deep within me. . . .

As I fought, it was like my body *remembered* moves. Like I had been programmed to fight in a past life or something. My arms and legs shot forward automatically.

"Find the strength within you! Call it forward!" Mr. Koto shouted. I could see him in the far corner watching me.

While I was distracted, Kenji's hand came down with a chop against the side of my neck. Pain seared through me like a laser blast.

But the agony seemed to make me fight better.

I swung my leg around like a whip and stomped down against Kenji's ribs.

Kenji reeled, flying backward against the wall. As he braced himself for support, he grabbed hold of one of the weapons hanging from the wall. It was a flat metal circle, with jagged edges like a saw blade.

I stood there frozen as Kenji flung it like a Frisbee, right at my head. . . .

Alien Terror
Alien Blood

Available from MINSTREL Paperbacks

Alien Terror

by
Chris Archer

A
MINSTREL®
BOOK

Published by POCKET BOOKS
New York   London   Toronto   Sydney   Tokyo   Singapore

A MINSTREL PAPERBACK *Original*

A Minstrel Book published by
POCKET BOOKS, a division of Simon & Schuster Inc.
1230 Avenue of the Americas, New York, NY 10020

mindwarp™ is a trademark of Daniel Weiss Associates, Inc.
Produced by Daniel Weiss Associates, Inc., New York

ISBN: 0-671-01482-X

First Minstrel Books printing October 1997

10 9 8 7 6 5 4 3 2 1

A MINSTREL BOOK and colophon are registered trademarks of
Simon & Schuster Inc.

Printed in the U.S.A.

Chapter 1

Telekinetic power or solar energy beams?

I heaved the ice chest onto the table, trying to decide which mutant superpowers I'd rather have.

If I were Professor X, I could just stand here and move the cooler with brain waves. But Cyclops could blast it with an energy burst from his eyeballs. Then again, he'd probably warp the plastic and boil the Gatorade inside. Still, Cyclops had the rad sunglasses and the red-headed girlfriend. He was my first pick.

I plopped down onto Coach Williams's folding chair and reached across the table for my comic book.

In front of me, a few of Metier Junior High's star wrestlers were already practicing illegal vice grips. They were scattering the mats I'd just spent fifteen minutes rolling out. Not that anybody cared.

"Yo, dweeb head!" Drew Molinari called out. He

1

was one of the team's biggest wrestlers and my personal enemy. "Gatorade!"

Drew didn't exactly score high in vocabulary, seeing as he confused "team manager" with "personal slave." He made up for it with brute strength, though. He tossed his opponents like a gorilla plucking out a flea.

Drew sort of reminded me of a thirteen-year-old supervillain. He had the build of an eleventh-grader, the face of a riled rottweiler, and breath that smelled like a cafeteria chili dog. Drew, the Incredible Bulk.

And me? I'm Ethan Rogers, the invisible kid. I couldn't actually disappear, but I was the type that blended into the furniture. People didn't really notice me much.

"Now, dork face! Not next Tuesday!"

That is, unless they feel like bossing me around.

Feeling kind of miserable, I pushed my comic book aside and fished a Gatorade from the cooler. It wasn't that this practice was any worse than usual. It's just that today was my birthday. My thirteenth birthday. And even though birthdays always turn out kind of lame, you can't help hoping they'll be special, anyway. I walked over to Drew and held the drink out to him.

"Open it," he ordered. Behind him, his three friends, Eddie, Larry, and Mick, nudged each other and snickered.

I held the slippery bottle and tried to twist off

the lid. But the sweat from my palm made it impossible to grip. Drew and his buddies elbowed each other and guffawed as my hand slipped for the second time.

If only I had Wolverine's claws, I thought. *I could open bottles and cans with a flick of my index finger while destroying my enemies.*

Finally I grabbed the hem of my "Vampires Suck" T-shirt and managed to twist off the cap.

"Here," I mumbled, handing over the neon green drink. My voice was weak, but my imagination was in full throttle.

LITTLE DID THE **EVIL MOLINARI** KNOW, BUT HIS DRINK CONTAINED A LETHAL AMOUNT OF KRYPTOMIUM NITRADE, WHICH WOULD RIP APART NERVES AND BLOOD VESSELS LIKE THREADS OF A SPIDER WEB.

"You sure you should drink that, Drew?" one of his bone-headed friends asked. "You might catch his wuss germs."

"Yeah, and I bet he just finished picking his nose," another one said.

Drew smiled menacingly. "No sweat. If I taste anything nasty, I'll just spit it in his hair. Might even improve the style."

Drew's friends howled at his joke. Then, just as

Drew lifted the bottle, Coach Williams banged open the steel gym doors and marched in.

AND SO THE **EVIL MOLINARI** AVOIDED HIS DATE WITH DEATH THANKS TO THE ARRIVAL OF A SECOND ENEMY, THE DREADED **SCREAMER**.

"All right, men! Line up! Put your drink down, Molinari! Hey, kid, get to work straightening these mats! Come on, come on. Let's move, men!"

Coach Williams was always calling his star athletes "men." He called me "kid," on account of my weighing in at ninety-eight pounds and looking about as muscular as an earthworm.

As Coach Williams took roll, I hustled around the floor picking up towels and straightening the mats. When I reached the area behind Drew, he purposely stepped backward onto my hand, crunching my fingers with his size-eleven Nikes. Coach Williams's booming voice drowned out my gasp.

"Harrison! Harrison!" he was yelling. "Where the heck is Harrison?"

"He's out sick, Coach," someone mumbled.

"Sick? He can't be sick! No one can be sick! We have our first meet next week and we need all the practice we can get!"

He marched up and down the row of wrestlers, glaring at each one as if he could bully them into pulling Harrison out of their pockets.

"In that case," he said finally, "kid, get over here and line up with everyone else. Now!"

"What?" I whispered. A dozen pairs of blood-thirsty eyes shifted in my direction.

"You heard me! A manager has to give as much as the players. And since we're short a team member, you're promoted. Line up!"

I couldn't believe it. Forget about hoping for a special birthday. Now I was just hoping I would get through it alive.

I threw the armload of gym towels onto the nearest bleacher and walked to the end of the line, right next to Drew.

What does Coach think he's doing? I wondered miserably. *I'll be pulverized!*

My knees threatened to buckle as Coach Williams went down the line pairing up the wrestlers. Eventually he reached our end.

"Rogers and Molinari! Take the center mat!"

Drew snorted.

"But, Coach," I argued. "I'm wearing jeans and I—"

"Shut your trap and move! Whatsa matter? You a member of this team or not?"

I walked dejectedly to our mat. Drew loomed behind me, sneering and cackling like a rabid hyena.

If only I were Dr. Draconian, I could swallow some of

those radioactive protein pills and triple in size and strength.

"All right, men! We're going to start with a few takedowns—just like we practiced last week. Get into starting position!"

Drew, being such a sweet guy, let me take the aggressor stance. He chuckled deviously as I stood over him. Why hadn't I paid any attention when the moves were taught? Probably because I figured I'd never need to know them.

Coach blew his whistle. Around me, ten other players gave halfhearted attempts with their moves—they were too busy staring at our mat.

Images of comic-book heroes flashed through my mind, and I leapt into action, jumping on Drew with all my strength. I was like a mosquito bouncing off the windshield of a two-ton diesel.

The next thing I knew, the gymnasium whirled around me, and I came crashing onto the mat.

"One . . . two . . . three!" counted a sinister voice.

Every nerve in my body throbbed, and strange, twinkly lights danced in front of my eyes.

"Keep it going! Keep it going!" Coach Williams ordered.

Before I could take a breath, I was yanked to my feet only to be slammed down again a second later.

"One . . . two . . . three!"

I was up, and again I came hurtling down.

"One . . . two . . . three!"

Up down. Down up.

"One . . . two . . . three!"

I couldn't take it. My body felt like liquid. I tried to focus my eyes on Drew, but everything looked red and underwater. I tried to beg for mercy, but I couldn't get my breath. Drew pinned me, flattening me under his mammoth weight.

"I haven't even broken a sweat," he jeered.

Suddenly, as I lay there smelling Drew's rancid breath and listening to the laughter of his buddies, my body seemed to revive itself. It was as if millions of cells instantaneously shook off the pain. My senses went back to normal and a strange feeling of power ran through my limbs. Relaxing and concentrating, I realized that Drew's weight was shifted all wrong—too much of it supported by his arms. Somehow I knew that a quick jolt above the knees would—

Whommmppp!

In a flash, I threw Drew off of me, flipped him around, and hurled him onto the mat.

"One . . . two . . . three!" I heard the voice before I realized it was coming from my own mouth.

The gym was deadly quiet. The other wrestlers froze. Coach Williams stopped hollering, his jaw dropping to his collarbone.

"Wha—? You? How did—? Get offa me!" Drew sputtered furiously.

AND THE **EVIL MOLINARI** GAVE UP IN OBVIOUS DEFEAT.

I figured it had to be luck. Pure, divine, incredible luck, possibly owing to my thirteenth birthday. No way could I actually throw Drew Molinari. I didn't have enough strength to toss one of his shoes, let alone both shoes with him attached.

Still, it happened. The whole team, including the coach, saw me do it. And Drew wasn't happy.

"You're dead meat," he had hissed in my ear when I finally let him up.

Coach Williams seemed kind of freaked out, too. He made everyone do stretches for the rest of practice and told me I could go.

So I grabbed my comic book and headed out to the front of the building to wait for my ride. After a few minutes, the thrill evaporated, replaced by the more familiar feeling of fear.

A chilly breeze cut all the way through my jacket. Overhead, the early evening stars illuminated the inky gray sky. I tried to read under the dim streetlamp, but my thoughts kept going back to my own battle with evil.

Maybe I had turned Drew's own energy against him, like Bishop in *The Time Lord's Mission*. Or maybe the ghost of tenth-level paladin invaded my body.

"Nah. You just caught him off guard," I mumbled

to myself. It was bad enough that the toughest eighth-grader in Metier, Wisconsin, wanted to crush in my skull. I didn't need to add delusions of super-power to my problems.

"Well if it isn't our manager." Drew's voice came from behind me. "Don't let my little spill back there make you think you're hot stuff," he snarled. "I lost my balance is all. You were just there to land on me." Drew said it as if he was trying to convince himself, too.

"I'm sure that's what happened," I mumbled.

"What did you say? You making fun of me?" Drew snapped.

His friends stepped out of the shadows and closed in around me.

"No, what I said was—"

"How about you and me settle this right here? How about we have ourselves a rematch?" Drew took off his jacket and pushed up the sleeves of his sweat-shirt.

"But . . . there are no mats," I pointed out.

"Oh, really?" he said sarcastically. "The manager must have forgotten."

As Eddie, Larry, and Mick circled around like vultures, Drew grabbed my collar and yanked me off the ground, pressing me up against the wall of the building.

"Payback time," he called out.

It occurred to me to mention that this was not one

of the takedowns we had learned, but I decided not to. Squinting my eyes and taking a breath, I braced myself.

HUNGRY FOR VENGEANCE, THE **EVIL MOLINARI** AND HIS GANG OF THUGS POUNCED ON OUR UNSUSPECTING HERO. NOW IT WAS HOPELESS. WHO WOULD RID THE CITY OF CRIME, CORRUPTION, CURFEW VIOLATORS?

"Look out! It's the cops!"
"Let's get out of here!"
Instead of Drew's meaty fist pulverizing my left cheek, I felt my rear end collide with the concrete sidewalk. I opened my eyes in time to see four burly guys disappear around the side of the building. A police cruiser pulled up to the curb.

JUST AS THINGS LOOKED BLEAK, A GALAXY-CLASS BATTLE CRUISER DROPS OUT OF WARP INTO THE FRAY. OUR HERO IS SAVED . . . **BY HIS RIDE**.

Picking up my comic book, I struggled to my feet and walked sheepishly toward the squad car.
"Hey, Dad," I said, opening the passenger-side door.

Chapter 2

"So, how was practice?" my dad asked as we drove out of the school parking lot.

"Fine."

"Is the team going to be ready for the big meet next week?"

"I guess."

"And how were your classes today?"

"Fine," I answered, fiddling with the buckle of my seat belt. Even if I wasn't strapped into a dark squad car with protective glass and bars all around me, I'd still feel trapped sitting there talking with my dad. We're not exactly the warm, fuzzy, chip-off-the-old-block father-son team. In fact, our conversations went like a worn-out script: his same questions and my same single-word answers. We were like figures in a boring video game stuck in level one.

About now he'll ask if I'm hungry.

"Are you hungry?" my dad asked. Score twenty points.

"Yep."

Now he'll say, "Mom has dinner ready."

"Mom has dinner waiting." Slight change in wording—score only ten.

"Great."

"Spaghetti tonight. And birthday cake," he added, with some emphasis.

"Oh? Sounds good."

Where's the magic button that'll reveal the secret exit out of here?

It wasn't really my dad's fault that things were this dull. I was the one to blame. It must have been tough on him having a son with no outstanding talents to brag about, especially since Dad had been such an all-American kid.

People still talk about when Burt Rogers played football for Metier High School. I guess no one has come close to his rushing yardage record since.

My dad's always trying to get me to play a sport, but I'm too small for football, too slow for basketball, too clumsy for baseball, and too smart for hockey. I don't even like watching the big games on TV. My dad made a big deal about me volunteering to be manager of the wrestling team to fulfill my gym requirement. It hasn't made me like sports any more.

One time, Dad tried taking me along on a hunting

trip—that's his other big pastime. I couldn't set up my tent, refused to shoot a rifle, and got yelled at for spraying insect repellent. At least, since I sat and read the whole time, I didn't scare off any targets. Later, though, when Dad picked off his first rabbit, I almost barfed at the sight.

That's another thing. I'm a vegetarian, and my father can't understand it at all. My dad honestly believes you are what you eat. You probably would believe it, too, if you saw my dad and me together. He's tan and beefy like a freshly grilled steak, and I'm about as thin as a celery stalk and as pasty as a garbanzo bean.

So, with sports, hunting, and chili cheeseburgers out as conversation topics, the stuff my dad and I have in common could fit under your fingernail.

Fortunately for him, I'm adopted—so he doesn't have to blame himself for how I turned out. Too bad adopting a kid isn't like ordering takeout. Dad could have specified he wanted a strong, muscular, meat-eating boy, preferably already dressed in a Green Bay Packers jersey.

As for me, I've always wondered if somewhere in Wisconsin there were two thin, pale English professors missing a son.

"*Bzzzt! Bzzzt!* Car fourteen. Car fourteen. Chief, do you read? *Bzzzt! Bzzzt!*" The police radio crackled like a popcorn popper.

Dad picked up the intercom. "I'm here, Carla. What's up?"

"*Bzzzzzt*. We've been getting all sorts of calls here. Apparently people keep seeing strange lights over the reservoir. Should I send a cruiser? *Bzzzzzt!*"

I looked out my window toward the western sky, where the reservoir lay just beyond the pine-covered hills. More strange lights? Ever since I could remember there have been reports of UFOs in the sky over Metier. The town is obsessed by it. Every few weeks someone calls up to report a flying saucer or weird flashes of light. Occasionally people even call 911 about alien creatures poking around their toolshed or levitating their cat.

My dad thinks it has something to do with the name of the town. Metier was settled by French-Canadians way back when, and everyone is supposed to pronounce it "met-ee-ay." Instead, folks just say "Meteor," which does give a kind of cosmic feel to the place. In fact, the reservoir itself was supposedly created by a giant meteorite back in prehistoric times or something. My dad figures all this local history makes people want to see UFOs so badly that their minds play tricks on them.

Personally, I wished the sightings were true. I would love to see a UFO.

"Negative on that, Carla," Dad said. "I'm sure these folks just left happy hour at Nicky's Bar. Don't waste any manpower following up, and disregard any further calls."

"Roger, Chief Rogers. *Bzzzzzt! Bzzzzzt!*" The radio burped and then went silent.

14

"Hey, Dad. Why don't we drive over and check it out? It's really not too far out of the way."

"No, son. It would just be a waste of time."

"But aren't you curious?" I asked. "What if there really is something there?"

"No, Ethan. It's just a bunch of lonely people making crank calls. It's best to ignore it. Besides, your mother is waiting."

"Okay," I mumbled. I figured Dad was right, being an experienced police chief and all. Still, the possibility of seeing a UFO, no matter how unlikely, sparked my imagination. I sighed and looked back out of the window.

OUR HERO GAZED UP AT THE NIGHT SKY WITH HIS TELEBIONIC VISION . . .

"Did I tell you your mom made spaghetti?"

. . . DESPERATELY SEARCHING FOR NEW SIGNS OF LIFE.

For dinner Mom made my favorite pesto sauce to go on the noodles in addition to the meat sauce for her and Dad.

Normally she doesn't go to all this trouble. Normally I have to make do with extra helpings of mashed potatoes or coleslaw while my folks devour some kind of roasted carcass. But today was special. I was no longer a kid. As of this day I was an official "teenager."

Somehow, though, I thought I would feel more . . . different. I guess I expected to morph automatically into a taller, stronger version of myself. Or wake up with a new, cool teenage attitude. Instead, I was me. Just like I was the day before, only a few hours older.

And forget privileges. I even had to do my regular chores of setting and clearing the table. After spending most evenings lugging coolers for Coach Williams and arranging place settings for my mom, I was beginning to wonder if I was destined for a career in a hotel.

BY DAY OUR HERO SPENDS HIS TIME AS A MILD-MANNERED BELLHOP. HIS SUPERHUMAN STRENGTH ALLOWING HIM TO LIFT MOUNTAINS OF LUGGAGE, AND HIS EXPERIENCE FLYING OVER THE CITY ON HIS NIGHTLY ROUNDS ALLOWING HIM TO GIVE EASY-TO-FOLLOW DIRECTIONS TO ANY TOURIST ATTRACTION.

"Ethan, honey. Would you like some more cake?" my mother asked as she sliced through the word "Happy."

"No thanks, Mom."

"Burt?"

"Well, maybe one more," Dad said, helping himself to the "Ha."

I wiped fudge frosting from my mouth and stood up to clear away my dishes.

"Wait, Ethan," my mom called. "Your father and I have a surprise for you." She looked over at Dad and proudly set a flat box in front of me.

My mind instantly calculated the dimensions of the box. My hands shook. My heart thumped. About a cup of sugar coursed through my veins. The box was roughly nine by twelve inches—the perfect size for a vintage comic book. Could it be? *The X-Men #1?* For two years I had been saving for it. Now it was going to be mine!

I tore off the wrapping and yanked off the lid. My fingers dug anxiously through the tissue paper, probing deeper and deeper. Finally a small beige business card fell into my lap. I held it up and read it. "Danny Koto's Karate School," it said in big, block letters.

My heart sank. My hands felt leaden.

"Karate?" I asked.

"We've enrolled you in self-defense class," Dad said through a mouthful of cake. "A boy should be able to take care of himself. It's a dangerous world out there. Look what happened to that Aldridge boy."

Todd Aldridge was a kid in my class. Last summer he disappeared without a trace. People searched everywhere. His photo was on the news every day for weeks. At school we had special assemblies on safety. Some people say Todd was abducted by aliens. My dad says he suspects "foul play."

"Your first karate class is tomorrow afternoon," my dad went on.

"It'll be so much fun, honey," my mom said excitedly.

"Yeah. Sure."

Just what I didn't want. Another way to embarrass myself. Another way to be harassed by people who were more athletic than me. Why couldn't we just rewind and start this birthday over? Why couldn't I just beam myself, particle by particle, into a new, more exciting dimension? Someplace where kids could get out of P.E. by scoring high in *Mortal Kombat* and where they always get exactly what they want on their birthdays.

I stared down at the card in my hand and then up at my parents' smiling faces.

"Thanks, guys. This is great," I forced myself to say.

"Oh, honey. I'm so glad you like it," Mom gushed. "Now how about some more milk?"

WARNING! YOUR LIFE FORCE HAS BEEN DRAINED. GAME OVER.

Chapter 3

The next morning was sunny and incredibly bright, but I was in a dark mood. I felt like Batman in the Dark Knight series: sullen and mopey, barely able to grunt a greeting to the perky people on the bus.

I wished I could live like Batman. Wear a mask, dress in black, drive a cool car, and have a servant take care of all the boring stuff. I wanted to crawl into a deep, dark cave for a while. Especially if it had an outlet for my Sega Saturn.

AS HE STEPPED OFF THE BUS, OUR HERO SURVEYED THE BATTLEFIELD BEFORE HIM— **JUNIOR HIGH**. HE WRAPPED HIS CAPE TIGHTER AROUND HIS BODY AND ENTERED THE LAIR OF THE EVIL AND OBNOXIOUS.

I squinted against the morning sun and made my way toward the front entrance of the school. I was supposed to meet my best friend Gary Beck in the library. He was going to help me cram for our test in Mr. Holland's science class.

Gary is a whiz in science. Seriously. He could probably teach the class if he wanted to—which he doesn't. He could probably do a better job than the teacher.

Mr. Holland is okay. I mean, he isn't one of those dried-up, burned-out zombies whose only joy in life is to hand out detention slips and *F*'s. But he just talks too much. And he never varies his voice at all. It's like listening to elevator music.

Anyway, Gary is always reading up on science—for *fun*. He's probably the only one who pays attention to Mr. Holland's endless lectures. The too-cool-for-school kids are always making fun of Gary, saying he tries to be the teacher's pet. They call him Mr. Holland's Dopus.

Anyhow, I do okay in science, but I always miss out on important details in class. I can't help it. Mr. Holland goes on about how to identify some vile substance, and I start thinking up an adventure about *Amoeba Man! Able to swallow entire cities in a single gulp!* Gary always fills in the gaps in my notes.

"Well, well. If it isn't the weightless wonder," Drew Molinari called out as I passed the schoolyard.

Speaking of vile.

Drew and his buddies always hang around the courtyard in the mornings playing a game called "Whip-It." That's where they chuck a racquetball as hard as they can against the side of the school building. Occasionally they knock the glasses off an innocent bystander or give a concussion to a curious pigeon. It's the perfect sport for Drew—mean yet simple.

"Hey! How did you get on the bus today, Pencil Boy?" Drew went on. "Did you walk through the door or just slide under it?"

Normally I just keep walking, maybe even speed up a little. Not today. Today I was the Dark Knight.

I stopped cold, turned, and stared right into Drew's doglike face.

He stared back into mine.

WITH HIS RADIOACTIVE, FLESH-SEARING, DEATH GAZE, OUR HERO LOCKED EYES WITH THE **EVIL MOLINARI**. . . .

"Ooh. He's asking for it," one of Drew's followers jeered. Eddie, I think.

"What's the matter? You gonna cry?" another one called. Mick, I think.

Gritting my teeth, I turned back around and pretended I didn't care. My blood simmered as I heard them laughing behind me.

Suddenly, a weird prickly sensation snaked up the left side of my head. With lightning reflexes I didn't know I had, I whirled around.

I snatched the racquetball out of the air—inches from my face—and turned to Drew.

"You should be more careful with your ball," I snarled at Drew.

I shot the ball back at the group. It whizzed past them like a blue rubber bullet and wedged into one of the diamond-shaped holes of the chain-link fence.

Right next to Drew's stunned face.

"I heard it was shaped like a hot-dog bun and had big blue lights on it."

"No. They said it was round, like a saucer. Don't you know anything about UFOs?"

"I heard it had big red lights."

"The lights were green. The lights are always green."

All day long at school people kept talking about the flying saucer reports from the night before. At lunch, Gary and I sat with our friends Bentley and Willy, comparing all the rumors.

Gary and I have been buddies since kindergarten, and since then we've added two more guys to our little group. Truth is, we were known as the science geeks, the Dungeons and Dragons fanatics, the Trekkers, the Myst conquerors. We analyzed facts. We memorized entire screenplays of our favorite movies like *Monty Python and the Holy Grail*. While other kids went skateboarding or flipped each other on wrestling mats, we surfed the net and flipped pages of comic books.

Today we were talking about the possibility of extraterrestrial life in Metier, Wisconsin.

"I'm telling you, it's possible. Don't you think it's weird that people keep seeing things over the reservoir?" Bentley Ellerbee said.

Bentley is a science fiction expert. He subscribes to *Omni*, knows the Starship Enterprise's schematics (second only to Scotty), and claims he has on-line chats with Kurt Vonnegut.

"My dad says it's just people's imaginations going wild," I said. "But I think there's something going on. Have you noticed that it's not always the same people saying they see the lights? How do you explain that?"

My expertise is action heroes. Of the four of us, I have the biggest comic book collection and I developed the coolest warrior in our D&D game. And I usually win the arguments over whether Spiderman could whip Magneto or the other way around.

"It's true!" Willy McIntyre said. "Mrs. Mulligan, that bleeping cafeteria lady, used to laugh at all the kids who talked about the sightings. But I heard she called the police station last night."

Willy is a walking Gameboy. He spends most of his waking hours manning his Super Nintendo as if he was the chief of a nuclear submarine. You name the game, he has it, he's played it, he's dissected its manuals, and he's scored higher than anybody you know. I think all those video games might be warping his brain. He uses the word "bleeping" a lot. Sometimes he runs around chairs and benches as though it's going to rack him up extra points.

"Well, I think there might be some other, more plausible explanation for these lights other than little green men from outer space," Gary said. "Maybe atmospheric phenomena or a disturbance in the earth's magnetic fields." Like I said, Gary's a regular Bill Nye.

"Still, don't you think it's funny that anytime there's a sighting, something weird happens?" I asked. "Like that time everyone spotted the lights and the next day all those machines and video terminals at the Metier Mall started going haywire. Then there was the big sighting last summer. Right after that, Todd Aldridge vanished."

We all nodded solemnly. Todd lived next door to Bentley. They had worked out every last strand of the *X-Files* conspiracy. His disappearance hit really close to home.

"Maybe these aliens are like scientists from another galaxy," Bentley said. "Maybe they've come to get samples of life from our planet. You know— dogs, cats, chickens, spear grass . . ."

"Teenagers?" Gary added. "You think that's what happened to Todd?"

"Well, yeah. I mean, maybe," Bentley said.

"Man, if that's true, why couldn't they take someone like Drew Molinari," Willy grumbled. "Someone people wouldn't miss much."

I looked over toward the school yard. Drew and the rest of his gang were in the middle of another "Whip-It" game.

I thought about telling my friends what happened that morning. The weird way I knew the ball was coming toward me, the way I grabbed it out of the air and threw it back really hard. The look of surprise—even fear?—on Drew's face . . .

But I decided not to. I'd had enough teasing for the week. Besides, I was beginning to wonder if I even remembered it right. Maybe comic books were warping my mind the way game disks were warping Willy's.

"I think you're wrong, Bentley," Gary said. "If aliens wanted good samples, there are much better spots on the planet with more varied forms of vegetation and animal life. Besides, we don't have any proof this is the work of extraterrestrials. Like I said, there could be a logical explanation. Seismic activity, swarms of insects—"

I groaned. This was the last thing I felt like talking about after just finishing a science exam.

"But think about it, Gary," I said, looking at the line of trees that ran from the school-yard fence down to the reservoir. "How cool would it be to see an alien?"

OUR HERO GAZED OUT AT THE **FORBIDDEN ZONE**, THE PLACE NO ONE DARED TO ENTER. SOMEHOW, IT SEEMED TO BE CALLING HIM.

Chapter 4

After school I was supposed to go to Danny Koto's Karate School. The class was in the Metier Mall, and I had my choice of transportation to get there.

I could take the school bus that drops off the kids that live downtown, including Drew Molinari and his terrorist friends. Or I could walk through the forest across the road from school, circle the reservoir, and end up a block away from the mall.

I stood in front of the bus circle, weighing my options. Let's see . . . teasing, wedgies, and possible bloody nose on the bus. Or the chance of running into a few of Metier's legendary aliens and a death-ray blaster or two if I went around the reservoir.

ONCE AGAIN, THE **FORBIDDEN ZONE** CALLED TO OUR HERO.

"Dad would kill me if he found out," I mumbled to myself.

My dad was always warning me to steer clear of the reservoir. I don't think it had anything to do with the UFO reports. More likely he was afraid of human evildoers hiding out in the forest. Either that or he was worried about the fragile environment of the watershed area. I kind of doubted that.

"Hey, Drew. Look! It's geek man!" Eddie (or maybe Mick?) yelled from the front of the bus line.

Drew turned and fixed his steely eyes on me. Suddenly I pictured myself being shoved out a small rectangular bus window and having my head sheared off by a tractor trailer.

I decided to risk death rays.

Shouldering my book bag, I trudged across the street and slipped through a rip in the chain-link fence.

A couple of yards into the forest and I couldn't hear the familiar buzz of voices or smell the diesel fumes from the buses. The forest was still and quiet. Kind of eerie, actually.

To my left, the path sloped down toward the inky waters of the reservoir. To my right, the trees and brambles crawled up the dark hillside. And in front of me, a worn path curved around the lake.

WITH HIS INSTINCTIVE TRACKING INSTINCTS AND SUPERHEIGHTENED SENSES,

OUR HERO TOOK NOTE OF HIS SURROUND-INGS, BOLDLY VENTURING INTO THE NEW ENVIRONMENT.

For some reason, the temperature seemed colder in the forest. Daylight was shut out by the canopy of branches overhead, and a dank, mossy smell filled the air. Everything was weirdly silent. I couldn't hear any birds chirping or the wind through the trees. All I could hear were the leaves crunching under my feet.

And then I heard a branch break close behind me.

My footsteps started giving off weird echoes.

Then I wondered if they might not be echoes at all. What if I was being followed?

Another twig snapped right behind me.

Someone is here. Someone is watching me.

Panic clenched my stomach. My breath escaped in rapid, shallow gasps, and every hair on my body stood up.

Then more new sounds: my heart pumping like a revved-up V-8 engine, and my Reeboks accelerating over the forest floor.

I ran as fast as I could, stretching every extra millimeter into my stride. But with each step, I could still hear the muffled footsteps behind me. At times it felt as if there were fingers—or claws—or tentacles— snatching at my back, raking across my coat.

If only I were Nightcrawler, then I could teleport myself out of here. Or if I had Storm's powers, I could vaporize whatever is following me with a few bolts of lightning.

Why didn't I just take the stupid bus?

Eventually, the path led me to Central Avenue and the Metier Mall. Once I saw the opening in the trees, I threw my upper body forward as though I was reaching for an imaginary finish-line tape. I was free!

I slowed down. But I didn't look behind me until I reached the road.

Scanning into the trees and brambles I saw . . . nothing. No antennae poking up from a bush. No acid-dripping tongues dangling from an oak branch. No scaly claws waving at me from behind a boulder. Not even a high-school student skipping school. Just a forest.

I shook my head and laughed—only I couldn't really laugh because I was so out of breath.

Those dumb UFO stories had really gotten to me. Had I actually been scared by a little echo and some twigs scraping across my back? Boy, my imagination could sure jump overboard fast.

SHRUGGING OFF THE EFFECTS OF THE **GURGO-SCRAMBLER MIND PROBE**, OUR HERO STRODE ACROSS THE BUSTLING AVENUE. HIS NEW MISSION WOULD TAKE HIM TO THE MYSTICAL LAND OF MINIMUM WAGE—**THE MALL**.

I still had a few minutes before Mr. Koto's karate class started, so I stopped by Planet X, the big comic-book store at the far end of Metier Mall.

The store was probably my favorite spot on earth. It was absolutely beautiful. Wall-to-wall bins brimmed over with plastic-sheathed comic books. Shelves were crammed full with sci-fi paperbacks, collector cards, and D&D modules. Every modern mythical character you could think of, from Arc-Angel to Zaphod Beeblebrox, lived there.

I loved that place. The musty smell of paper. The bright colors of the superhero posters tacked up everywhere. The sound of Mr. Winfrey's hacking cough.

Mr. Winfrey is the owner—a real nice guy. In fact, he reminded me of a cartoon character himself. Sort of like Elmer Fudd with a New York accent. He had the same doughy face, cherry-tomato nose, and bald round head.

I was the only person under the age of twenty that he let hang around in the store. I think he was impressed by how much I knew about vintage comics. We understood each other in a way that only comic-book freaks could.

Every weekend I came by to read, hang around, have discussions with Mr. Winfrey, and stare longingly at the thing I wanted most in the world: *The X-Men #1* in mint condition.

Gary is always teasing me about how long I've

saved for it, especially since it's so out of date and the characters aren't drawn up as beefy and muscular as they are now. I don't care. It would complete my collection. And besides, in twenty years it'll probably be worth twice as much.

Truth is, though, I wanted it for other reasons, too. I know it sounds dorky, but my heroes were born in *The X-Men #1*. It was like a passport that would bring me closer to them. Mr. Winfrey understood. He kept it up front in a display case instead of in the safe with the other valuable editions. That way, I could see it whenever I wanted to.

OUR HERO APPROACHED THE PRICELESS TREASURE. HUNDREDS HAD DIED FOR THE SACRED TEXT. WARS HAD BEEN WAGED FOR IT. PHILOSOPHIES HAD BEEN BUILT AROUND IT. GLANCING INTO THE FRESHLY WINDEXED CASE, HE SAW . . . **AN EMPTY PEDESTAL!**

The comic was gone! The metal stand was empty.

"Oh no! Mr. Winfrey!" I looked around the store. "Mr. Winfrey?"

He was standing in the back, right next to the cardboard cutout of C3PO. Next to him, a man in a business suit was leaning over one of the bins with a comic book open in front of him. I glanced at the pictures as he thumbed through the pages. I'd know them anywhere. He was looking at *my* comic book.

As I stared at the guy, a funny feeling crept over me. And not just because he was handling my comic book. It was as though I was picking up a signal from the guy.

He looked normal enough. Tall. Dark hair. Mustache. Still, something told me not to trust him. Maybe it was the way he flipped the pages, not even bothering to look at the pictures. Maybe it was the way his tie was knotted so tight under his chin—it looked as if it was keeping his head attached.

Whatever it was, I knew there was something dangerous about him.

WITH HIS GENETICALLY ENGINEERED AUDIOTRONIC HEARING, COMPLETE WITH **TWENTY-FIVE SWITCHABLE CHANNELS**, OUR HERO LISTENED IN TO THE CONVERSATION.

"Four hundred fifty, huh?" the man said. "Are you sure that's your final price?"

"You ain't at no flea market, fella," Mr. Winfrey said. "That there's the going price. Take it or leave it."

The man rubbed his greasy palm over his chin. "Well, I guess I could swing that. But I'll have to come by tomorrow with the money."

Mr. Winfrey was going to sell him my comic? No way! He'd probably wall it up in a safe-deposit box for years. Or choke it to death in some kind of frame.

"We open at 10 A.M. tomorrow morning. And I don't take out-of-town checks," Mr. Winfrey added.

The man handed the comic back to Mr. Winfrey. "Don't worry," he said mysteriously. "I'll get cash."

My spine tingled as the man brushed past me and headed into the mall. Something definitely weird was happening. It was as if I had Spiderman's special warning sense. For some reason, my whole nervous system was screaming at me to be wary of this guy.

No two ways about it. I couldn't let him buy my comic book.

"Hey, Ethan! Howsa bouta new read, eh?" Mr. Winfrey said, turning toward me.

"Mr. Winfrey, you *can't* sell him that comic. Please don't!" I begged.

"Sorry, kiddo. I know ya had yer sights on it. But I'm in the money-makin' business, ya know?"

"But I'll *give* you the money. I will! I can have it tomorrow! Promise me you won't sell it."

Mr. Winfrey looked at me. He smiled and shook his head. "Sure thing, kiddo. But ya gotta get here before this other guy."

"No problem," I said. "Thanks, Mr. Winfrey."

Actually, there was a problem. A big one. Where was I going to get the money?

34

Chapter 5

Danny Koto's Karate School was on the other end of the mall. It was a huge, gymnasium-sized room with mirrors on the walls, a dark green mat covering the floor, and a door and a giant front window facing Orange Julius.

Great. Now anybody who wanted could get a ringside seat for my big karate debut.

ATTENTION METIER SHOPPERS . . . ATTENTION METIER SHOPPERS . . . PORT-O'-PETS IS HAVING A SALE ON GERBILS— BUY TWO, GET SIX FREE . . . JETHRO'S CDS AND CASSETTES IS FEATURING GREAT YODELERS OF THE ALPINE NATIONS . . . AND FOR YOUR VIEWING PLEASURE, A SKINNY THIRTEEN-YEAR-OLD WILL DISLOCATE

EVERY ONE OF HIS LIMBS AT KOTO'S KARATE SCHOOL.

Walking into the studio, the first thing I noticed was that I was much older than all the other kids. They looked as though they'd be more interested in *Sesame Street* than learning martial arts.

The second thing I noticed was that Mr. Koto looked ancient. I figured he had to be at least eighty years old. He was only my height and had pure white hair. The skin on his face had so many tiny creases, it looked like a piece of paper that had been crumpled up. The way I saw it, he should have been at home watching *Diagnosis Murder* and drinking Ensure. What was he doing teaching twelve rug rats self-defense?

"Ah yes. Rogers boy," Mr. Koto said as I approached him. "Welcome to our class."

He gave me a slight bow and then handed me a uniform like all the other kids were wearing. White cotton jacket, loose pants, and a white woven belt. Everyone trained barefoot. No shoes or socks allowed on the mat.

I went to the bathroom to change and checked my reflection on the way out. I looked like I was wearing a pair of baggy pajamas. I lined my shoes up next to a bunch of pairs of Ninja Turtle sneakers. I felt like I was at a second-grade slumber party.

"My favorite's Donatello," I mentioned to a boy standing next to me. He just stared back blankly and wandered off to join the others. Kids today. No sense of irony, you know?

I walked onto the mat and lined up with the rest of the class.

WITHOUT HIS WEATHER-RESISTANT, BULLET-REPELLING CYBERHIDE SUIT, OUR HERO STOOD STRIPPED OF HIS SUPER-POWERS . . .

"Hey! Look who's playing dress up with the preschoolers!"

. . . AND HIS **PRIDE**.

Just my luck. It already felt as if my ego had been diced up and skewered like shish kebab. Now fate sent a couple of Drew Molinari's idiotic friends to watch. Larry and Mick gawked at me through the wide-screen window, their ugly faces squished against the glass and their laughter floating in through the open door.

I tried to hide behind other kids, but it was impossible since I towered over everyone. Weird. Finally I was in a place where I'd be considered big and all I wanted to do was shrink down to the size of an Ewok.

As the kids formed into neat rows facing the window, they didn't even seem to notice Larry and Mick. Suddenly I had a horrible thought. What if Mr. Koto paired us up for a few fighting rounds and I got my butt kicked by a kindergartner? I would have to commit hara-kiri on the spot.

Before I could weigh my options, Mr. Koto walked in front of the group and bowed, signaling the beginning of class. The students bowed back.

"Feel the forces around you," he said, sounding like Obi-wan Kenobi in *Star Wars*. "Move with the energy."

Luckily, instead of finding a partner to start wailing on, the other students began this series of moves. In total synchronization, they circled their arms and lifted their knees in a weird kind of dance. I tried to follow along as well as I could.

Drew's friends started laughing hysterically.

Nobody, including Mr. Koto, seemed to notice. I guess they were used to the occasional wise guy.

"Flow with the power," Mr. Koto said.

Like little zombies, the kids stretched, turned, and reached their arms around in a slow arc, as if they were pulling aside a curtain. My gestures seemed jerky and stiff in comparison.

I was amazed at how seriously these kids took their karate lessons. None of them were slacking off or joking around like I would have expected.

Larry and Mick should be taking notes. These kids might be small, but they could teach those idiots a thing or two.

Mr. Koto walked up and down the rows of students, calling out instructions—only instead of barking out demands like Coach Williams, he made hokey animal metaphors in a calm, mysterious voice.

"Be like the tiger," he said.

I could barely resist pointing my finger in the air and shouting, "They're grrreat!"

"Be like the falcon."

Did he want us to flap our arms?

"Be like the dragon."

Yeah. I guess breathing fire would be a good thing to know.

"Be like the monkey."

Okay, this was getting silly.

Finally the sequence ended and we stood at attention.

"And now," Mr. Koto said, "we show the power of the empty hand."

"Yiiiaaah!" the class yelled in unison. I almost jumped out of my baggy pants.

Immediately each student began alternating their arms in full-force punches. Their legs lunged, their fists shot out against the air, and they made that brain-rattling cry.

"Yiiiaaah! Yiiiaaah!"

I couldn't believe how expert these little guys were with the movements. They looked like an army of

Rock 'Em–Sock 'Em Robots. I tried my best to copy them, but judging by the laughter coming from Drew's friends outside the window, I probably looked pretty silly.

So this was my birthday gift. An hour of humiliation in front of my worst enemies. Not exactly on a level with *The X-Men* first-edition comic book.

That's when it occurred to me. Maybe I could make a trade.

I could make up some excuse and ask Mr. Koto for a refund after class. That way I could get enough money to pay Mr. Winfrey! I knew my dad would be furious, but I'd think of some way to explain it to him.

Knowing this was going to be my first and last karate class made me not worry so much about technique. I followed along halfheartedly with the exercises, daydreaming about my prized possession.

Almost as if he was reading my thoughts, Mr. Koto looked right at me and waved me over.

"You must yell when you strike," he said as I walked up. "Voice cries as hand flies. Do it again, with the yell."

Man, this was embarrassing.

"Eehaw?" I called out as I thrust my arm forward.

"No. Like this. *Yiiiaaah!* Now you try."

"Ya."

"From here," he said, poking me in the belly. "Yiiiaaah!"

"Yah!"

"Good. Much better."

At this point, two hefty-looking older guys came into the room. They were wearing similar jackets and pants as we had on, only their belts were black. Mr. Koto nodded to them and they walked off. When they came back, they stood off to the side, carrying a huge concrete brick between them.

I figured it was probably some kind of endurance test. Be like the sawhorse or something.

Mr. Koto clapped his hands. Immediately his students stopped their drills and knelt down on the mat. I followed.

"Story time!" one of Drew's friends shouted. Why couldn't they go to the arcade instead?

I looked at the faces of the little kick boxers around me and tried to imagine them face-to-face with a third-grade version of Drew Molinari. Would knowing all these moves really help them?

One thing was sure—I did not want to risk getting flung onto the mat by an eight-year-old. My pride would never survive it.

If I had to practice with anyone here, I hoped it would be Mr. Koto. I figured I could take him.

"Be like the snake," the old man chanted, raising his withered arms in a fighting stance. "Find a weakness, and *strike!*"

With supersonic speed, Mr. Koto suddenly shot out his leg and whipped his bare foot against the cinder block the big dudes were holding. Instantly, the brick disintegrated into rubble.

Okay. So maybe I couldn't take him.

"Mr. Koto? Could I talk to you a second?" I asked, coming up to him after class. "I was wondering. Um, I think there's some problem with my schedule and all, plus I kind of have a trick knee, and I sort of wanted to know if I could, um, maybe get my money back?"

"Yes," he replied without a hint of surprise. "Come follow me."

Maybe it was because he talked as though he was quoting from fortune cookies, but I half expected Mr. Koto to call me "Grasshopper." Considering how my arms and legs stuck out from the uniform, the nickname would have fit.

He led me to a long table in the far corner of the room. He opened up a small metal box, pulled out a stack of twenty-dollar bills, and started counting them out.

But just when Mr. Koto was about to put the wad of money in my hand, he stopped. In a quick, catlike move, he grabbed my hand and studied it intently. Then he stared into my eyes for what seemed like an hour and a half. His usual cryptic smile disappeared. Instead he looked worried.

What did I do?

"Please, come with me," he said, finally letting go of my hand. Something told me not to argue.

Mr. Koto took me through a mirrored doorway that

opened into another room. Inside, about ten guys who looked like Jean-Claude Van Damme were paired up in high-action, bone-crunching fighting matches. With incredible speed, they whirled their arms and legs, jumped around, and shouted so loud you'd think the floor was covered with scalding lava.

It was pretty cool.

A muscular guy was standing in front of the group. I recognized him as one of the two men who carried in the concrete brick. On the wall behind him, a bunch of exotic weapons were on display.

"This is my son, Kenji," Mr. Koto said as we approached the man.

Kenji turned toward me and bowed politely. I bowed back.

"Kenji is also karate master. This is his black-belt class," Mr. Koto went on.

Mr. Koto mumbled something to Kenji that I couldn't hear over the shouting. Then Kenji yelled out something and banged a huge gong that was standing in the corner. Immediately the fighters stopped. They bowed to each other, bowed to Kenji, and left the room.

"I will make you an offer, Rogers boy," Mr. Koto said, turning back to me. "If you wish to get back your money, you must fight Kenji."

"What?" I barely choked out the word.

I didn't hear him right. He didn't just say I had to fight Kenji.

I was sorry and all if I insulted Mr. Koto by wanting to get out of his class. But this seemed kind of severe.

I paused for a moment, waiting for somebody to laugh out loud and say "Gotcha!"

Instead, Mr. Koto took the gong mallet out of his son's hands. Kenji raised his arms in a fighting stance. As I looked into their faces, I slowly realized they were serious.

"Um . . . Mr. Koto. I can't fight him."

Mr. Koto just stared at me as if I was about to cry "Shazam!" and suddenly sprout a lot of muscles. I tried to explain.

"You see, Mr. Koto," I spoke as slowly and clearly as I could. It was starting to seem as though I was dealing with a couple of psychos who'd taken too many blows to the head. "Kenji is very big and strong and really good at karate. Right? And I'm skinny and slow and very new to this sport. There's no way I could fight him."

Mr. Koto's expression was stony.

"Besides, I'm supposed to be home soon."

Still no reaction.

"Look, if you don't have the money to pay me back right now, I could drop by some other time and pick it up. I come to the mall a lot. I'm always at the comic-book st—"

"It is not money we seek. It is truth!" Mr. Koto practically shouted. "You will fight Kenji. You will prove your determination. Then, win or lose, you will get your money."

I get it. This guy isn't going to really fight me. This is a test. This is only a test. If this was an actual fight, Kenji would already be strapping my molars to my femur bone and using it as a back scratcher.

All I have to do is make a halfhearted attempt and prove my determination. Then he'll stop the fight and pay me.

"I'll do it," I mumbled feebly, glancing at Kenji's muscular forearms.

"Good. Get into position. When you hear the bell, begin."

The old man stepped back several feet and struck the gong.

Chapter 6

"Yiiiaaah!"

Instantly, Kenji lunged toward me, striking out with his arms and legs.

I raced backward as quickly as I could, tripped, and fell on my butt.

"Feel your instincts!" Mr. Koto called out.

I am, I thought. My instinct is to run away.

"Remember the training," Mr. Koto went on. "Recall the animal within you!"

Right. Right. Be the lion. Be the bunny. Yadda, yadda, yadda. I still don't know what I'm doing.

Kenji stood poised in attack position, waiting for me to get back to my feet. As soon as I was upright, his foot slammed into the side of my head.

I collapsed again.

The room swirled. My brain throbbed.

Wait a minute. Kenji's really attacking me! A

couple more blows like that and I'll snap like a pencil!

"Feel the creature inside you! Listen to it!" Mr. Koto shouted.

As I lay there writhing and feeling as though I was going to heave, Mr. Koto's words suddenly made sense. I really could feel something stirring deep within me.

Something dark. Something really, really strong.

Looking up at Kenji's cool expression, I felt myself turn inside out.

It was weird. I can't possibly explain it to you. It was as if this creature inside of me came forward and the regular Ethan hid behind it. Suddenly my fear drained away. I wasn't thinking anymore—at least, not the way I usually do.

Before the Ethan part of me knew what was happening, I was on my feet, facing Kenji. Everything looked different. I know it's hard to believe, but it was as though my vision had widened. I could see Mr. Koto way back to my left, the doorway way back to my right, and Kenji looming in front of me. I could even see myself, or at least the front part of me, as I lifted my arms and bent my legs.

Kenji charged at me with a sharp jab, his knuckles flying toward my throat.

Time seemed slower with my weird new fish-bowl vision. From a safe spot inside me, the regular Ethan watched as he/I/it stepped out of Kenji's path, grabbed his arm, and sent him soaring upside-down.

I'm not kidding you. That's really what happened.

Like a cat, Kenji flipped back onto his feet and swung around with a high hook kick.

I ducked to avoid it, grabbed his knee, and sent him toppling over me.

With my IMAX vision, I could see Kenji behind me. He jumped back to a standing position, spun around, and came toward me, his arms flying like rotary blades.

"Yiiiaaah! Yahhh!"

I blocked his punches. I don't know how.

Then, as he came close, I jumped forward, kicking my legs toward his stomach.

Kenji sidestepped my kick and came at me again, arms and legs flailing.

Somehow I protected myself from each blow. Anytime I sensed an opening, I struck. But Kenji would always leap out of the way.

We went on like that for a long time. We were sizing each other up, matching each other's pace. I know it's hard to believe.

As I fought, it was as if my body *remembered* moves. Like I had been programmed to fight in a past life or something. My arms and legs shot forward automatically.

"Find the strength inside you! Call it forward!" Mr. Koto shouted. I could see him in the far corner watching me.

49

While I was distracted, Kenji's hand came down with a chop against the side of my neck. Pain seared through me like a laser blast.

But the agony seemed to make me fight better.

I swung my leg around like a whip and stomped down against Kenji's ribs.

Kenji reeled, flying backward against the wall. As he braced himself for support, he grabbed hold of one of the weapons hanging from the wall. It was a flat metal circle with jagged edges like a saw blade.

I stood there frozen as Kenji flung it like a Frisbee right at my head.

Now I was dead for sure.

I ducked just in time. As the object sailed past me, I could hear it spinning in the air. A super-high-pitched whine and a faint "whap-whap" sound. Then a dull "Chthunk!" as it dug into the opposite wall.

With my improved perception, I could sense Kenji's movement. I turned in time to see two more of the razorlike gizmos flying in my direction.

I quickly dodged the missiles and ran toward Kenji.

"Yiiiaaahhh!"

He met me with a powerful roundhouse kick.

"Hiiiaaahhh!"

I countered with a jab to his kidney.

"Eeeaaagh!"

Kenji crumpled against the display wall and then

came back at me an instant later with an ornately decorated knife in his right hand.

As he jabbed the four-inch blade at me, I leaped and ducked and sidestepped like a jump-rope champion.

Finally, when he brought his arm down in a vicious chop, I circled my forearm, collided the side of my hand with his wrist, and knocked the blade from his hand.

The dagger skittered across the floor. As I watched it go, Kenji blindsided me with his elbow and I went hurtling into the wall.

When my head snapped up again, I was staring at the wall—and at a long, curved samurai sword.

Impulsively, I reached up and pulled it out of its sheath. Holding the carved hilt in both hands, I waved the blade in Kenji's direction.

It was totally mind-boggling. The weapon felt familiar in my hands, and I swung it around like a pro.

Kenji saw the sharp point inch dangerously close to him and suddenly dove toward my feet, rolling toward me like a human bowling ball.

Without thinking, I jumped over him and pivoted back around to keep up my attack.

By trading places with me, Kenji was right next to the wall now. In the split second it took me to turn and charge, he had yanked down the other samurai sword and was whipping its cutting edge toward my abdomen.

Metal clanged against metal.

Our eyes locked.

For several crazy minutes, we leaped and lunged, whittled the air with our long thin blades, and slowly made our way around the room in a bloodthirsty dance.

Then, just as I was backing Kenji into a corner, he swung his sword in a wide, powerful arc.

I had no chance. With the force of a Babe Ruth home-run hit, he knocked my sword out of my grasp and sent it sailing across the room.

The Ethan inside me screamed in terror.

The creature that had taken over my body told me to chill.

Just as Kenji was swinging back around for the mortal blow, I did the craziest and most amazing thing of all. I jumped up with all my might, twisted in a back flip, and landed several feet away. With my su-perwide vision, I scanned the display wall for another weapon. I spotted a pair of nunchaku hanging there. I could also see Kenji racing toward me with his sword out, ready to skewer me.

"Haaaiiiii!"

In a flash, I pulled down the nunchaku and whirled around. Of course I'd never touched nunchaku in my life, but somehow I got them spinning in time to ward off Kenji's sword.

We fought more intensely than ever. The sword slashed the air. The nunchaku whistled and cracked.

We were locked in a battle that seemed to go on forever.

Suddenly a deep, blaring sound rippled through the air, shattering our concentration and freezing us in midair.

"Kwwwaaannng!"

Mr. Koto stood behind us, banging on the gong.

All of a sudden, I was me again. The creature disappeared and Ethan crawled out of his hiding place. Kenji, too, seemed as though he snapped out of a trance.

Our weapons clattered to the ground, and I collapsed, exhausted and out of breath. My senses had returned to normal—my ears buzzed, my head throbbed, and my body felt as if it had been mulched—and my super-surround vision and incredible agility were gone.

What is happening to me? What went on here? I was so tired I could hardly form the thought.

Kenji grabbed my hand, pulled me to my feet, and bowed respectfully. I bowed back, not too steady on my feet.

Then Mr. Koto came over and placed his hand on my shoulder. "You are very special," he said in a voice so soft I could hardly hear him over my breathing. "Henley's son. I knew your father."

If I was dizzy before, it was nothing compared to now. "W-what do you mean?" I stammered. "You knew my real father? But—but—who is he? Where is he? How do you know him?"

The old man just stared back at me, watching me closely with his wrinkly eyes.

"Tell me what you know," I pleaded. My voice cracked. "I need to know what's happening. Who is Henley?"

Instead of answering, Mr. Koto turned and headed out the doorway, into the front classroom. Kenji followed close behind him.

I staggered after them, too weak to keep up. My mind whirled with all sorts of questions and doubts. I was confused, scared, excited, and totally worn out.

"Wait," I called, gathering up my clothes and shoes and following them to the front room.

Mr. Koto turned around slowly and walked up to me. He pressed a wad of money into my palm and met my eyes with an eerie stare.

"You are in great danger," he whispered urgently. "Do not draw attention to yourself. Be like the snake. Remain still, hidden, cautious. Sometimes the best weapon . . . is restraint. Remember this."

Then he and Kenji disappeared through the doorway into the small office marked "private."

I stood staring at my reflection in the mirrored wall, searching for any clues that might explain what had happened to me.

AS OUR HERO STARES AT THE MYSTERI-
OUS FACE IN THE MIRROR, HE IS OVERCOME

BY A SUDDEN, SHOCKING REALIZATION THAT
HE IS ACTUALLY—

My imaginary captions faded.
Who needed to invent a comic-book alter ego
when you've just discovered your own real-life super-
powers?

AND SO THE HERO RETIRES HIS CAPE . . .
FOREVER.

Chapter 7

When I walked through the front door of my house, my mom took one look at me and shrieked.

"Goodness, Ethan! You're drenched in sweat!" she yelled, running over to feel my forehead. I was used to it. Anytime I clear my throat or my eyelids look droopy, my mom takes my temperature.

"Tough workout, eh, son?" my dad said, punching me on the shoulder. He was beaming.

"You could say that," I said.

My mom steered me toward the dining room. "Well then, come to the table, Ethan. We were starting to get worried."

"Yep. I'm sure you're really hungry after all that exercise," Dad said, settling into his chair.

Actually, I wasn't hungry at all. I felt empty, but not like I wanted food. Whatever happened back at Mr. Koto's studio left me so numb and tired that all I wanted to do was crawl under a rock and go to sleep.

"So, tell me about Mr. Koto," my mom said, spooning a big pile of buttered carrots onto my plate. "Was he nice?"

"Actually . . . he wasn't what I expected."

"What do you mean?" Dad asked.

"Well, he is really old. I mean, he must be about eighty-four or something."

"That's not important," my mom said, dumping a mountain of rice next to the carrots. "Senior citizens are as capable as everyone else."

"And he sort of pushed me into some . . . advanced fighting."

"That's good!" my dad said. "You'll learn faster that way."

"And he told me to be a tiger. Or an ox. Or a serpent, or something."

"That's nice," Mom said.

"Hmm. Must be a way of mentally preparing you to fight. Like those Olympic athletes," Dad said.

"Ethan, honey. You haven't taken a single bite of your food. Eat it before it gets cold," Mom said.

I stared down at my plate. The carrots looked soggy. The rice looked goopy.

I doubted I could chew anything at that moment, anyway. Not just because the meal looked gross, but because my teeth felt funny. A strange itchy sensation was running from my gums to the ends of my teeth. My eyeteeth especially tingled.

"I'm just not very hungry, Mom," I said, twirling my fork.

"Makes sense," Dad said. "Sometimes after a grueling game in football, I wouldn't be hungry for hours."

I watched as Dad took his fork and skewered a hunk of what had once been a bird of some kind. I wondered if he would be impressed, maybe even feel closer to me, if I told him what really happened at karate class.

But what really happened? Did I really fight a black belt? How did I know all those expert moves? How did I handle all those weapons? Did I imagine the whole thing?

And what did Mr. Koto mean about me being in danger?

Forget trying to explain it. I couldn't even think straight.

The old man's words echoed in my mind. "You are very special. . . . I knew your father."

"Dad, do you know anyone named Henley?"

Crash!

My mom dropped her teacup onto her plate. Dad froze in midbite. They stared at each other for a fraction of a second, passing a look of worry and shock.

"Uh, no," my dad said. He looked really uncomfortable. "Where did you hear that name?"

"From Mr. Koto. He called me Henley's son."

My parents looked at each other helplessly.

"Well, he must have been mistaken is all," Dad said.

"That's right," Mom said, leaping up from her chair and sopping up her spill with a wad of napkins. "I mean, you said he was old. He's probably senile. And if you ask me, I'm not sure he's fit to teach."

"He did keep you pretty late," Dad said suspiciously.

"And you look terrible—all clammy and pale. What is he thinking making someone your age work that hard?" My mom began clearing up the dishes as she talked, even though they had barely eaten their dinner and I hadn't touched mine.

"You know, I have half a mind to go down there and demand my money back," Dad said.

"You don't have to, Dad," I interrupted. "I already asked for a refund. He gave it all back to me."

"Well, good. You use it to get yourself something nice. That class is not for you," my mom said in a rush. She kept racing around the table, trying to erase any sign of our dinner. She was making my head spin.

"Um, Mom, Dad. If you don't mind, I think I'm going to bed early. I don't feel too good."

My mom's hands flew to my forehead so fast she almost gouged my left eye with a sticky butter knife. "You're sick, aren't you? I knew you didn't look well the minute I saw you. You poor thing. Really, Burt, I think you should consider investigating that man."

"Calm down, Lois. Let the boy get up. He'll be all right."

As I stood and walked out of the room, I could feel them watching me closely. The silence was suffocating.

It sounds strange, I know, but it was almost as if I could feel their fear.

For a long time I couldn't fall asleep. I lay there in bed listening to my mother's shrill voice and my father's bellowing bass as they argued downstairs.

I couldn't make out what they were saying, but they were talking about me. I knew it.

No matter how hard I tried to get comfortable, my body wouldn't unwind. The room seemed too bright, and even though I was under three layers of blankets, I felt cold. Plus, I still had that weird tingly feeling in my teeth.

Eventually I put my pillow over my head, curled myself up, and drifted off. . . .

I'm back at the reservoir. I'm running, but my body feels as if it's wrapped in lead.

Something is after me. I can hear footsteps and a strange hissing noise behind me. I'm trying to race through the trees, but it takes so much energy just to lift one foot, I end up plodding along like a rusty robot.

The noises grow louder. Whatever's chasing me is closing in fast. I strain to shake off the heaviness, but it's no use. I'm trapped in an invisible cocoon of lead.

Suddenly, a gong sounds nearby. Mr. Koto appears in the path up ahead. He bows and points toward me with the gong mallet.

Instantly the cocoon bursts open. I can really move now.

The footsteps are directly behind me, but instead of running, I stop and turn. I see a tall man racing toward me. He's wearing dark clothing and a black hood tied over his face.

In a flash, he's on me, jerking his arms and legs in powerful karate moves. I dodge his blows as best as I can and throw a few sharp punches, but I can feel my body weakening.

I hear the gong again. All of a sudden, I realize I can make weapons out of random objects with a touch of my hand. A branch changes into a sword. Rocks turn into daggers. But still the black-hooded man avoids every one of my blows.

After an endless battle, the attacker finally knocks me to the ground and pins me with his huge arms. As I struggle, my hand accidentally pulls off the hood of my enemy.

Only he's not human. Instead, I look up to see a weird, twisted face staring back at me with big obsidian eyes.

"Aaah!" I jolted back awake, my arms flailing against the empty air.

My muscles were all tensed up and my head

pounded. Sitting up in bed, I was about to reach over and turn on a light, when I noticed my room was already lit up.

Everything looked strange. Glancing around, I realized I had my 270-degree vision back. Only this time it was even weirder. Even though it was the middle of the night and my overhead light was off, a bunch of the things in my room were glowing with a strange phosphorescence.

On my desk across from me, my Macintosh Performa gave off an eerie, neon blue light. The radiator in the corner flickered like the snowy screen of a television set. Looking down, I realized I could actually see the coils inside my electric blanket, pulsing like tiny fluorescent snakes. Even my own body was lit up with the blue-white glow.

What's going on? I wondered numbly. *Am I still dreaming?*

I reached over and flicked on the bedside lamp.

Blazing beams shot out from under the shade like a nuclear blast. The light was so bright, it seared my eyes. I quickly turned it off again.

The lamp was off, but the lightbulb kept glowing with the strange aquamarine light.

I got up to look around.

Maybe this is some kind of freak weather thing, like red clouds or yellow rain. Or maybe there's a problem with the electrical wiring in our house. I wonder if it's too late to call Gary. He'd know.

I opened the door of my room and stepped into the hallway. As I walked through the pitch darkness, a glowing blue-white thing suddenly scurried past my feet. It was Mom's cat, Heimlich.

How is it I can see him so clearly out here, but nothing else?

I followed Heimlich down the hall and into the bathroom. My dad always leaves the faucets dripping at night to keep the pipes from freezing. That's Heimlich's favorite way to drink water.

My hand shot up to switch on the bathroom light, but then I changed my mind. No reason to fry my corneas again. Besides, Heimlich lit up the place like a furry torch.

As I got to the sink where Heimlich was already lapping up the steady drips, I realized something. For some reason, the water from the cold spigot, where Heimlich drank, was invisible to me. But the water from the hot spigot shone like bright blue lava.

I can see heat! That's what all those glowing things had in common. I realized this without quite believing it. *The electrical appliances, the radiator, the water, Heimlich . . . me.*

I checked my reflection in the medicine-cabinet mirror. Sure enough, my face glowed blue like a ghost. But there was something weird about my eyes.

Reaching behind me, I flicked on the light. I squinted and blinked against the harsh glare. When my vision adjusted a little, I looked back at my mirror image. What I saw made my blood stop in my veins.

My eyes blinked back at me like jet black coals.

No! No! This isn't happening! My head was throbbing and I sucked in gasps of air.

There I was, looking just like the terrible thing in my nightmare. Only this time I was awake. Or was I?

I stood there paralyzed, staring at the horrible alien face in the mirror.

Then I watched the blackness in my eyes slowly shrink back into my regular-sized pupils. After a minute my eyes looked normal again, and my weird vision disappeared.

I splashed cold water on my face a few times. Then I turned off the light and headed back to my room.

The weird blue glow was gone.

I crawled into bed and lay there in total darkness, haunted by my own terrifying thoughts.

What is happening to me?

Chapter 8

I woke up early the next morning and the world felt almost normal again. The memory of my dream—or dreams, I guess—felt blurry and vague.

After all, the sun was shining, it was Saturday, and I had a routine to keep.

First I eat chocolate Pop-Tarts and milk for breakfast, grab a few game cartridges, and head over to Gary's house. Then Gary and I challenge each other to a few rounds of *Mortal Kombat* or *Zombies Ate My Neighbors* until the good TV shows come on. We always take a break to watch *Spiderman* and *The X-Men* before going back to the games.

If *Spiderman* is a repeat, we switch channels and watch a few classic Bugs Bunny cartoons. It's not like we're five-year-olds or anything. We watch them for important reasons.

Gary is working on a web site called "The Physics

of Warner Brothers Cartoons." He's already got lots of notes on the special scientific laws that rule the world of Looney Tunes. Here are some examples:

- A toon needing to run somewhere fast has to first churn his legs in place. When velocity is achieved, the toon can launch himself in any direction, leaving behind a curly white streak.

- When a toon is falling from a cliff, he won't drop right away. Instead, he'll pause long enough to hold up a sign that says "Eep!"

- Anytime a shovel or frying pan is whacked against a toon's head, the metal will take the exact shape of his face. That, or his head will reconfigure to the shape of the frying pan. (Researchers are still working on this one.)

- Anvils are everywhere, and they're usually falling.

As I rode my bike the few blocks to Gary's house, I yawned so hard I felt as if my face would crack. Maybe violent cartoons really could mess up your perception of reality. Maybe that was part of the reason I was seeing these strange things lately. Maybe it was time to tune into *Sesame Street* for a change.

"Welcome, Ethan," Gary said in his best Boris

Karloff impersonation when I walked into his living room. "Prepare to die."

I sat down beside him and picked up a set of controls. Nothing like Nintendo to help you forget your worries. The opening part of *Mortal Kombat* played on the television screen.

"Not this time, Gary. I feel lucky," I said. I always say that. Then I always lose.

Not only is Gary a superbrain in science, he's also supreme grand master champion at *Mortal Kombat*. He's amazing. It's the one game where he can even beat Willy McIntyre. As far as I know, no one has ever beaten him.

We chose our kombatants and Gary started the game.

"Eat my plasma, Idioticus Supremus!" Gary yelled, throwing a net of slime over my player.

I charged forward with a low fireball.

"Make out your will, Dorkus Maximus!"

Gary began his usual strategy of air throws, hammer punches, and teleporting. Being the technical maniac that he is, he loves any character that uses fancy gadgets. Like Cyrax or Sektor.

Not me. I'm kind of a purist. I like the martial arts warriors and street fighters—humans who fight by a code.

"Give us your liver!" he cried, using his best Monty Python accent. On screen his android launched a missile.

I dodged it and knocked him with a bicycle kick.

I couldn't believe it. I was actually winning. It was as though I had suddenly figured out the game, after all this time. I could predict Gary's moves and counter each one with the perfect gotcha grab or high-flying kick. Before I knew it, his energy bar had fallen dangerously low.

"Hey!" Gary shouted as I finished off his guy. "What's with you today? Did you get a hold of a secret moves manual or something?"

"Uh-uh." I shook my head. "Guess I'm just more focused or something. I had an extra Pop-Tart this morning. Maybe that's it."

We started a new round. Within a few seconds my karate master had his sorcerer on the ropes.

"Aaargh!" Gary yelled as I crushed his guy. "I can't believe you just did that!" He stared at me in amazement. "Who are you and what did you do with the real Ethan Rogers?"

I laughed and shrugged my shoulders, but inside I was beginning to wonder. I really wasn't much like myself lately.

Gary growled and threw his control pad in frustration.

Ethan, two games. Gary, zero.

We began another. This time I held back a little. It was boring when the fights ended too quickly. Besides, Gary was starting to lose his cool.

I watched him as he played, his eyes scrunched up and shoulders tensed. Always calculating.

He's playing all wrong, a voice inside my mind said. *The trick is to relax and follow your instincts. He's thinking two moves ahead. I'm thinking of what I want from his refrigerator after I whip his butt.*

Funny. I was starting to think a lot like Mr. Koto.

My dream from the night before came back to me a little more clearly, and I remembered the strange blue lights in my house. A prickle of fear started in the bottom of my stomach.

"Um, Gary, have you ever heard of someone being able to see heat? You know, like seeing a glow from anything that gives off warmth?"

"Heat-sensing vision," he said without taking his eyes off the screen. "Sure. I've read about that in technical magazines. You need special goggles for it. Special forces in the military use it to track the enemy."

"Really? You have to have special glasses?"

"Yeah. Either that or be a reptile. Reptiles can naturally see thermoenergy. It's a survival technique since they need to absorb heat from other sources."

"But can people have that type of vision? Without the goggles, I mean?"

"No," he said, a little irritated. "Not unless you're Superman. Why?"

"Oh, no reason. Just wondering."

"You and your comic books. Aw, man! That's the game!" He shook his head and leaned over to eject the cartridge. "Oh, well. The shows are coming on in a minute anyway. I think *Spiderman*'s a rerun, so what do you say we watch some Bugs? I'm working on a theory about how the characters in Marvin the Martian cartoons breathe in outer space."

I glanced at the wall clock. It was nine-thirty. "Sorry. I've got to run a really important errand up at the mall."

"The mall? Can't you do it later?"

"No. I've gotta get to the comic-book store right when it opens." *And after that I'm gonna try to get some information out of Mr. Koto*, I added silently.

"You and your comic books," he mumbled again.

"Hey, maybe we can meet up with Bentley and Willy later on at the arcade. I'll have a surprise to show you guys. We'll play the X-Men game and I—"

"I know, I know. You'll get to be Cyclops," he said, shaking his head. "I can't believe you beat me today. How did you do it?"

I pushed open his front door and headed outside. "That's my secret. Never question the forces behind the all-powerful Shao Kahn. Heh, heh, heh."

"You're dethpicable!" he yelled in his best Daffy Duck voice.

Yep. Cartoons really could mess with your mind.

I pedaled to the mall as fast as I could. I had to get there before Mr. Winfrey opened the shop. I didn't want to risk the creepy stranger arriving ahead of me and buying my comic book.

Life was sweet. I'd had this incredible—weird but definitely incredible—experience at Mr. Koto's karate school yesterday. I beat Gary in *Mortal Kombat*. I finally had the money for my treasure, and I had plenty of time to make it to the mall before the stores opened. Finally, after all this time, I would take home *The X-Men #1*.

I shouldn't have gotten my hopes up.

Just as I left our neighborhood and pulled into the bike lane along Central Avenue, I rolled over something sharp. The blowout made me go crashing sideways into the rough gravel.

My right side stung a little from the impact, but I was madder than I was hurt. Now I would have to walk the bike all the way to Metier Mall. I was afraid I might not make it there before the other guy.

He doesn't deserve the comic book. I'm the one who's been saving money for two years. I'm the one who visited it all the time. If he gets it, I don't know what I'll do.

After twenty minutes of pushing the bike, I reached the mall parking lot.

My heart plummeted when I saw that Mr. Winfrey's van was already there. It was easy to spot. There was a cardboard cutout of Darth Vader sitting in the passenger seat, and the license plate read "XCOMIX."

"Please, please, please don't let me be too late," I whispered.

I locked up my bike and sped into the mall, down

the corridor, right up to Planet X. The lights were still off inside the store and the gate was only halfway up.

I did it! I made it in time!

I reached for my wallet and pulled out the stack of bills I had already clipped together. I couldn't wait to get my hands on my comic book.

"Mr. Winfrey!" I called, ducking underneath the gate. "It's me—Ethan. I have the money like I promised!"

"Good. You're just in time," someone said.

Only it wasn't Mr. Winfrey's voice.

I walked up to the front counter where two shadowy figures stood by the cash register. I could make out Mr. Winfrey in the dim light, but I didn't recognize the other guy—the one who was talking to me.

He turned and flashed me a mean grin. He had a black mustache and was wearing a shiny tie.

The man from yesterday!

I was just about to plead with Mr. Winfrey to sell me the comic, when I felt an invisible hand clamp around my windpipe.

The man was holding something in his right hand. Something that looked an awful lot like a knife, and it was pointed directly at me.

I'd just walked into a robbery.

"Hand over the cash!" the man demanded, waving the knife for emphasis.

"D-do as he says there, Ethan," Mr. Winfrey coaxed.

By now my eyes had adjusted to the semidarkness. I noticed the cash register drawer was open, completely empty. Mr. Winfrey's gold watch was gone and a bunch of collector-edition comics were poking out of a leather attaché on the counter.

Dread knotted my intestines as I glanced over to the display case. Just like yesterday, the pedestal for *The X-Men #1* was empty. The man was taking it, too.

"No!"

I don't know what I was thinking. I guess maybe I wasn't thinking at all. I leaped onto the robber and tackled him. I caught him completely off guard, and, for a few seconds, he lay there under my knees.

"Ethan! Watch out, boy!" Mr. Winfrey yelled.

The robber must have still had the knife in his hand, because a blunt object struck me on the side of my head. The pain was staggering. I groaned and fell sideways into a magazine rack.

As I lay there, stunned and writhing, something big happened.

Like the day before, a creature inside of me came forward. And my regular self hid in a storm cellar of my mind.

My special vision powered up in time to see the robber scramble to his feet and point the knife at me. Before he could come at me, I yanked the aisle rug out from under him, knocking him off balance.

I faced him. He stared back at me, terrified.

"Your eyes," he said.

He backed away from me slowly and knocked against a bookshelf. Pewter figurines came raining down on us. I managed to catch a statuette of Merlin the size of a football. I sent it spiraling at the robber's arm—the arm that held the knife.

The sharp point of Merlin's hat pierced the robber's jacket and he shrieked in pain. He fell backward, but he kept a tight grip on the knife.

I charged forward at him, and then it was as though time slowed to a crawl.

He looked up at me, raising the knife.

I felt the blade pierce my side, then everything went black.

Chapter 9

I remembered a blur of sensations. People shouting. Sirens. The motion of an ambulance. More voices. Poking and jabbing. Beeps and buzzes. My mother wailing. Dad barking out orders. Bright lights . . .

Someone was shining a small flashlight into my eyes.

An official-sounding woman was saying something about a possible head injury.

Then Mom started bawling again.

I wanted to talk to her. I wanted to tell her I was okay. I wanted to tell her to be quiet because my head hurt.

But I couldn't move. It felt as if I was wrapped in iron—just like in my dream.

I'm dying! That's it. It's all coming back to me now. The robbery. The fight. The knife . . . I was stabbed!

"No!" I cried out. Only I didn't make a sound.

No way was I going to die. Mom and Dad would kill me if I died. Besides, I had too much to live for. I never got my comic book, I'd just mastered *Mortal Kombat*, and I needed to find out some answers from Mr. Koto. Like what was happening to me? And who was Henley, anyway?

"No!" I shouted again. This time I actually created sound waves. It sounded like "Mmmmfff."

The unfamiliar female voice was explaining something about "delayed effects of trauma."

"Doctor," my father's voice interrupted. "Doctor, I think he's coming around."

"I'm not!" I yelled loud and clear.

My mom looked as if she was going to faint with relief. "You're not what, honey?" she asked, her fuzzy image hovering over me. "I'm here, Ethan. So's your father. Talk to us. Tell us what happened."

"I'm not going to die," I said stubbornly.

My mom glanced up frantically toward a blurry figure in white.

Then a strange woman's face appeared before me, beaming a flashlight into my eyes again.

"Hello, Ethan. My name is Dr. Strickrichter," she said. "Do you know where you are?"

"No."

"You're in the hospital. But it looks like you're going to be okay. You have some bruised ribs, a bump on the head, and a large contusion on your left side. Other than that, you're perfectly fine."

"The knife," I said weakly, sitting up in the bed. "I was stabbed."

My mom and dad exchanged fearful looks.

"No, Ethan. You weren't stabbed. You were just banged up pretty badly, that's all," Dr. Strickrichter said.

Dad stepped up to my bed. His face looked haggard. "Son, we did find a knife at the scene. And Mr. Winfrey claims to have seen it. Can you tell us what happened?"

"I'm telling you, I was stabbed! Right here, in my side." I lifted up my hospital gown and pointed to the place just below my left ribs. But instead of a bloody mess, there was only a round, pinkish bruise—about the size of a half-dollar.

How can that be? I remember the knife. I remember the blade ripping into my body and shocking me into unconsciousness.

"I'm not lying," I said emphatically. "I remember it."

Again, my parents looked over at Dr. Strickrichter worriedly.

"Sometimes head injuries can cause a patient to hallucinate. This is probably a temporary effect of the trauma his brain received. Still, I'd like to admit Ethan for observation overnight just to be sure."

"But I feel fine," I said. "Really."

Mom put her hand on my forehead. "Ethan, sweetie. The doctor only wants to make certain you're okay. Besides, it's just for one night."

"Someone will be by soon with some papers for you to sign, Mr. and Mrs. Rogers. I'll check on Ethan later on. In the meantime, if you need me, you can have me paged at the front desk," Dr. Strickrichter said. Then she turned and walked out of the room.

"Ethan," Dad began after she left. "I need to know what happened back at the comic-book store. They've already questioned Mr. Winfrey and studied the store video monitor. I have to say, it sounds pretty incredible."

"You didn't really fight that man with the knife?" Mom asked.

"He was trying to rob Mr. Winfrey," I explained.

"That's no excuse," Dad bellowed. "What you did was very stupid, son. You could have been killed."

"You were very lucky. You could have been stabbed," Mom echoed.

But I did get stabbed. Something weird must have happened. Could I have healed myself instantaneously? Like Wolverine?

I lifted the hospital gown again and pressed against the sore spot. It hurt, but it sure didn't feel as if a blade tore into me there.

I have to get out of here. I have to see Mr. Koto and make him answer my questions. I feel as if I'm going crazy.

"Are you the Rogers family?" a high school–aged candy striper asked, poking her head into the room. She was gorgeous. Black hair. Big dark eyes. Husky

80

voice. She reminded me of Catwoman without the mask.

"Yes," Mom said. "That's us."

"I have some forms for you to fill out." She handed a clipboard over to my mother. Then she turned toward me.

"Are you Ethan?" she asked in a low voice.

"Um, I'm, uh . . ."

"Excuse me?"

"Y-yes," I finally choked out.

She walked up to my bed and set a flat cardboard box on my lap. "This came for you at the front desk."

"Thanks," I said breathlessly, staring into her almond-shaped eyes.

"You're welcome. My name is Yvonne. I'll be looking in on you this evening. If there's anything I can do, press that orange button next to the bed." Then she turned and floated out the door.

Then again, maybe staying overnight won't be so bad after all!

"Who is that from?" Dad asked, pointing to the box.

I studied the container. It had my name written on the outside, but otherwise there were no markings or labels. "I don't know," I said.

"Well, open it up, honey," Mom said. "It's probably from one of your friends."

I lifted off the top and found a small white card. It read:

To Ethan:
   Thanks for everything. You're
my superhero.
                    —Mr. Winfrey

Then I carefully separated the tissue paper and uncovered a mint-condition comic book: *The X-Men #1*.

Later that night, I finally got some time to myself.

It seemed as though I spent the whole afternoon and most of the evening talking to people: my worried parents, who made me promise I wouldn't make a habit of fighting armed robbers; a police investigator, who treated me like royalty since I was Chief Rogers's son; and a couple of doctors, who mainly wanted me to track a red ballpoint pen they waved in front of my face.

After a while I started to get a little tired and a lot perturbed. I wanted to read my comic book and savor it page by page, but there was always someone in my room.

Eventually, Yvonne came back and chased everyone out, saying I needed to get some rest. Dad had to practically drag Mom home, after he swore they would come back first thing in the morning and Yvonne promised to call if my condition changed.

"Try to get some sleep," she said, switching off the lights.

"Actually, I thought I'd do some reading first," I

said. "Do you think you could leave the lights on for a little while?"

"Hmm. Brave defender of justice and a reader, too. I'm impressed," she said with a smile. "Well, okay. But if you're still awake when I come back, you'll be in big trouble."

She flashed another knee-weakening grin before slinking out of the doorway.

So this is the life of a crime fighter. Warding off villains with one hand and women with the other. Hmm. That's pretty cool. Maybe I could get myself a mask and a cape. Sew a catchy emblem onto a shirt. Come up with an alias. Let's see . . . the Kombat Kid? Planet-X Man?

Weirdly though, my conscience spoke to me in a voice that sounded like Mr. Koto's. "Do not draw attention to yourself. . . . The best weapon is restraint!"

Killjoy.

I reached over and picked up my comic book. I lovingly turned each page and soaked up every picture. It was mine! All mine! I was complete. I was happy.

I was staining the paper with my sweaty palms.

"Argh!"

Quickly and carefully I put it back in its plastic sheath. I figured I could look at it later after my hands were washed, dried, and sanitized.

Only now I was bored. I still wasn't ready to go to

sleep, but I didn't have anything to do. No magazines. No handheld video game. Not even a phone so I could call up my friends and tell them about my big adventure.

A small television was mounted on the wall across from me. I switched it on with the remote control and caught the tail end of a monster movie.

It could have been any one of the hundreds I'd seen before. A young couple, covered in the muddy stains and bloody scrapes, stand there holding each other passionately. Music swells. Viewers weep. I begin a silent countdown.

"Ten, nine, eight . . ."

Sure enough, just as the lovebirds are driving off in their sporty red convertible, a hideously decayed zombie grabs them from behind.

Bloodcurdling screams. Screeching violins. And the credits start rolling.

Why are people in horror movies so stupid? Doesn't anyone think to check the backseat?

I was about to switch stations when the Channel Three ten o'clock news came on. Martin Treadweather, the phony-faced news anchor, greeted the folks of Metier with a smirk.

"Good evening. I'm Martin Treadweather and this is Channel Three's evening report."

Duh.

The chintzy theme music faded as the camera zoomed in for a close-up. Treadweather's waxy face assembled itself into a serious expression.

"Our top story is one that will shock and amaze you."

Yeah. Right. Tell it to your hairdresser.

"Tonight we bring you startling video footage of a local teenager foiling a crime in progress."

What?

Suddenly I saw myself on screen. Somehow, they got a hold of last year's school yearbook portrait. Talk about a crime. I was about two inches shorter, still had my braces, and a haircut from hell.

"Thirteen-year-old Ethan Rogers, son of Metier Police Chief Burt Rogers, entered Metier Mall's Planet X Comic-Book Store this morning and found a burglar holding store owner Morty Winfrey at knifepoint. In an incredible show of heroism, Rogers managed to subdue the armed suspect and thwart the attempted robbery. Channel Three has obtained taped footage of this extraordinary act."

They began rolling the tape from the store's monitor. The picture was a little fuzzy because of the distance and dim lighting, but it was me all right. It showed me overpowering the robber and tossing him over my shoulder like a garbage sack. Then there was the flash of a knife blade.

When the lens refocused, the next few seconds of footage knocked me speechless. Since I had no memory of what happened after I got stabbed, I was seeing it all for the first time. It was kind of like watching a Jackie Chan movie, except with a pale scrawny kid as the star. There I was, wailing on the guy with a series of kicks and punches—expert karate moves that, until yesterday anyway, I had no idea I could do.

Amazing. Totally and completely amazing.

The tape showed the man struggling until I knocked him out with a head butt.

Sorry, Mr. Koto. So much for my showing restraint.

The camera cut back to Treadweather's face.

"Both Rogers and the assailant were taken to Metier Mercy Hospital with minor injuries. Hospital officials tell us that Rogers is in good condition and expected to make a full recovery. The suspect has since been apprehended and identified as Yeager Rudd, a known con man wanted in three states on charges of robbery and fraud. We will bring you more updates on this story as it progresses."

Unbelievable. I'm a TV star. A local hero. A dude to be reckoned with.

Again Mr. Koto's words sounded in my head: "You are very special."

I guess I am.

"In other news," Treadweather's nasal voice continued, "Akira 'Danny' Koto, karate master and long-time resident of Metier, died in his sleep last night at the age of one hundred."

_____Chapter 10

When I arrived at school Monday morning, I felt like a completely different person. I was battle scarred. I was the proud owner of a rare and valuable comic book.

And I was popular.

On the bus, so many kids packed themselves around my seat, I was worried it would flip over from being lopsided. It seemed like everybody had seen the footage of me on the news.

"All right, Ethan!" called out Ben Jameson, our class president, as I walked up the front steps of the school.

"Way to go, Ethan!" Lynette Barbini, our school's head cheerleader, whooped.

"You're the man!" a couple of total strangers shouted.

It was kind of overwhelming being the center of

so much attention. To be honest, I felt a little like a fraud. But after a while, I got into it. I gave everybody what they wanted. I swaggered around like a movie star, showed some slow-motion fighting moves when they asked, and worked up some answers to the questions that people kept asking. "Nah. I didn't have time to be scared. I just reacted."

While I stood there talking to my admirers and demonstrating a chop block for Lynette Barbini, I noticed Drew and his ape-men leaning against the courtyard fence, watching me. They were the only ones who hadn't congratulated me.

Guess they'll have to find someone else to pick on, now.

Eventually I made my way to the lunchroom. Gary, Bentley, and Willy were sitting at our regular corner, eating greasy cafeteria food and debating stuff as usual. It was weird. I felt as if I hadn't seen them in years. They seemed exactly the same as always, but I felt completely different.

As I joined them, I waved to a nearby table of girls who were pointing at me and whispering.

"Hey, hotshot," Gary said.

"Man, Ethan, everyone is talking about you. It's like you're the next Batman or something," Bentley said.

"We kept trying to call you yesterday, but your mom said the doctor ordered total rest. I guess she thought we'd make you get all hyper," Willy explained.

"Yeah. I spent the whole day eating her homemade split-pea soup and drinking apple juice," I grumbled.

"So, come on. Tell us everything," Gary urged.

They leaned forward expectantly and I gave the whole blow-by-blow account of my busting up the robbery. Well, not exactly the *whole* story. I left out the part about me getting stabbed. I figured since I didn't have any gaping wounds or missing limbs, I'd have a hard time proving it. And I didn't want them to think I was exaggerating.

"I can't believe you challenged an armed criminal," Gary said when I finished the story. "That has to be the stupidest thing you've ever done."

"Still, it was probably the coolest thing you've done, too," Bentley said.

"Yeah. How did you learn all those fancy moves?" Willy asked.

I shrugged uneasily. That was the question I couldn't answer.

Luckily Willy came up with his own answer. "Do you get pointers from all those comic books you read?"

"Oh, sure," I said casually. "Speaking of which, you're never going to believe what I brought with me today."

I unzipped my backpack, pulled out one of those padded mailer envelopes, and carefully removed a heavily wrapped, flat object. After unwrapping two layers of tissue paper and three plastic sheaths, I triumphantly held up *The X-Men #1*.

"The comic book! You finally got it!"

"Cool! How much did it cost you?"

"Can I see it?"

I checked their fingers for crumbs before handing it over.

"Mr. Winfrey just *gave* this to you?" Willy asked, shaking his head. "Man! Next time you need to rescue someone, let's go to Circuit City. We'll load up!"

"I'm telling you, Ethan, if you keep slapping around the local criminals, it won't be long before someone makes a comic book about you," Bentley said.

Now that *sounded good.*

Just then, Mrs. Haskell, our school librarian, came up to our table.

"Excuse me," she said, "but are you Ethan Rogers? The young man who helped catch that robber this weekend?"

"Um, yes," I answered.

"I just wanted to say that I think you did a very brave thing. It's nice to know our community has such courageous, upstanding young people. Your parents must be very proud."

Actually, my folks grounded me for a week, and I spent my entire Sunday listening to them lecture about the hazards of knives. The whole thing really freaked them out.

I decided to go with a lie instead. "Oh, sure. They're beaming."

"Well, they should be." She turned to go, then met Bentley's gaze. "Aren't you Bentley Ellerbee?"

"Sure am," he said proudly.

"Oh, I'm so glad I saw you. Listen, if I don't get *In Search of Bigfoot* by this Friday, I will need to collect $22.50 from you. Is that clear?"

Later that day, I sat in Mr. Holland's class trying to concentrate on his lecture.

". . . and so, by carefully crossing strain after strain of these pea plants, and investigating the slightest difference in traits such as color and height, Gregor Mendel came up with a theory on dominant and recessive genes . . ."

I yawned and looked over at Gary. He was taking pages of notes.

". . . we find that organisms displaying traits that help in their survival flourish. As new mutations arise . . ."

Mutations. Mutants. The X-Men.

Maybe Bentley was right. Maybe I could become a superhero. It wouldn't be so bad. In fact, foiling that robbery was the best thing that ever happened to me.

". . . genetic characteristics that help advance the species . . ."

All morning long people treated me like a star. I got high fives from popular kids. Girls who never noticed me before were oohing and aahing. Teachers were praising me as a role model. What wasn't to like?

If I could just learn how to tap into my hidden skills and use them whenever I wanted, I could start a whole new life.

". . . in the competition for food and procreation, causing the weaker strains to eventually die off and . . ."

I was kind of shaken when I heard that Mr. Koto died. I mean, he was super old and all, so what can you expect? But I was really hoping he could tell me what was happening to me, and teach me how to control these strange powers. Now that he was dead, I wondered if I'd ever learn the truth about my real parents.

". . . thus a new species emerges from the old."

Mr. Koto warned me to lie low and not draw attention to myself. But why? I liked the new me. I liked being someone special.

No one ever really noticed me much before. Not that I was a social outcast or anything, I was just . . .

". . . your basic square."

Mr. Holland turned and drew a big square diagram on the board. The movement caused the entire class—except Gary—to stop daydreaming. Whenever Mr. Holland put a word or diagram on the board, you could bet your lunch money it would be on the test.

Just as I began scrawling on my paper, a knock sounded on the classroom door.

"Excuse this interruption," Principal Lower said, poking his head inside, "but could I see Ethan Rogers? I'm afraid I'll be needing him for the remainder of the class period."

First my comic book. Then instant fame. Now a ticket out of Holland's class. Things keep getting better and better.

I gathered up my books and followed Principal Lower into the hallway.

"It seems you have a visitor," he said, smiling broadly.

"Really? Is it my dad?"

"No."

"My mom?"

"No."

I thought for a moment. "A girl named Yvonne?" I asked hopefully.

"You'll see," he said smugly.

He sure seemed to think I'd be excited about this person. Not that I trusted his judgment.

Principal Lower is one of those guys who is completely clueless about people under the age of thirty. He's always handing out lollipops, calling us "boys and girls," and suggesting we play stuff like hopscotch or marbles at recess. Once he caught a group of rough-looking high school students coming out of the woods across the street and actually believed them when they said they'd been fishing. I don't know what you need to have to be hired as a principal, but a clue isn't one of them.

"Go ahead and put away your things," Principal Lower said as we passed by the locker area. "You'll be going straight to lunch afterward. Oh, and you might want to get out your lunch box."

Lunch box? Get real.

After I shoved my bulging backpack into the mailbox-sized locker and squeezed the rusty lock shut, I followed Principal Lower to his office.

As soon as I walked in the room, a mouthful of gleaming, straight white teeth faced me like a miniature picket fence. For a second, I was blinded. Then the rest of the face came into view.

Martin Treadweather, Channel Three's Ken-doll news anchor, stood and held out his hand.

"Hello, Ethan. I'm Martin Treadweather, from Channel Three News."

Duh.

"Hi," I said, shaking his clammy palm.

"Our station has been covering the story of your incredible fight with the robbery suspect. I must say, we are all very impressed."

"Yes, Ethan is quite the hero around here," chimed in Principal Lower. "In fact, I'll be giving him a special certificate of recognition later today."

Oh joy.

"How exciting," Treadweather said. Then he

inched his face closer to mine. "So, buddy," he said in a NutraSweet voice. "Would it be all right if we ask you a few questions and give your adoring public the story of the man behind the myth?"

"Um . . . I guess so."

"Good!"

First Treadweather ordered a fat cameraman to get some footage of me and the "proud principal." You would have thought Principal Lower was getting a million-dollar check from Ed McMahon. He kept looking past me toward the camera, pumping my arm like a car jack, and saying schmaltzy things like, "This is a proud day for us at Metier Junior High."

Afterward, Treadweather thanked Principal Lower about a thousand times and asked if he could use the office to interview me privately.

"No problem. Take as long as you need," Lower said. Then he and the cameraman left the office.

Treadweather's toothy smile disappeared and his face arranged itself into a serious look.

"So," he began. "How long have you lived in Metier, Ethan?"

"All my life."

"And your parents are . . ."

"Burt and Lois Rogers. My dad is chief of police. Didn't you already put that in your first story?"

"Just double-checking the facts," he said matter-of-factly.

There was something weird about Treadweather—something besides his moussed hairdo and his fake tan.

Is it his eyes?

"Tell me, Ethan," he continued. "Have you always known how to fight like that?"

"Um, no. I mean, I wasn't born knowing how to throw a guy who's twice my size. Ha, ha, ha," I answered.

"Uh-huh." Treadweather was not amused.

Why isn't he writing this stuff down? Or videotaping it? And why did he chase the others out of here?

Suddenly warning flares began shooting off in my brain. It was the same uneasy feeling I got when I first met the robber at Planet X. Treadweather's questions were strange, and I didn't like the way he stared at me, as though he was probing my skull with his eyes.

"Um, don't you need my parents' permission to interview me?" I asked.

"Why? You're old enough to make your own decisions, aren't you? You're what? Thirteen?" He squinted at me. "In fact, you just turned thirteen recently, didn't you?"

How did he know that?

My internal security system immediately went into red alert, notifying the rest of my body. My heart sped up. My muscles were tense. I ordered my mouth to stay shut.

Treadweather leaned forward and met my gaze.

"Ethan, have you been going through any . . . changes lately?"

Brrrrriiiiing!

The alarm bells seemed to clang louder in my head. Then I realized it was the school intercom, signaling the beginning of lunch.

"Gee, Mr. Treadweather. I really enjoyed our interview," I said, using my own phony voice. "Unfortunately, it's time for my . . . headache medication. The doctors told me if I didn't take it with food, it could burn a big hole in my stomach. So, if you'll excuse me."

And I ran out of the office.

At recess that day, I still couldn't shake the dangerous feeling I got from Treadweather. My instincts had been right about the man in the comic-book store, so I knew I shouldn't doubt myself this time.

Why would Treadweather be so nosy about my family and me? There was definitely more to it than regular nosiness. For one thing, he seemed to know most of the answers already. How did he know I'd had a birthday recently? And how did he know about my new abilities?

Maybe there were some drawbacks to being a superhero.

"Wow. Martin Treadweather came to see you?" Bentley asked.

"Man, I think I'd risk a knife wound if it meant

getting out of Holland's class," Willy mumbled.

"Actually, I thought the lecture was really interesting today," Gary said. "Ethan, did you know that most mutation occurs quickly, as a result of big catastrophes rather than over the eons of evolution?"

"Sure, Gary. I think I saw that on an episode of *The Magic School Bus*," I said dryly.

"Well, you can see my notes if you want."

As we sat on a bench and talked, I could see the jocks starting up a game of Whip-It in the school yard. Occasionally, Drew Molinari would catch my eye, wrinkle his upper lip, and flash me a withering look.

Don't mess with me, Drew. Don't even think about it.

"Evolution, huh?" Bentley mumbled. "So, Gary, do you think if species keep evolving, animals will be able to talk someday?"

Gary shook his head. "Not likely. If they actually evolved to the point of talking, chances are they would evolve in other ways, too. So, we wouldn't even recognize them as horses or dogs or rats or whatever."

"What about Looney Tunes?" I asked. "Do you have a theory on how they can talk?"

"Well, actually," he began in an expert tone of voice, "most of them, like Porky and Daffy, have speech impediments. So, I guess the phonics are still beyond them. Plus, not all of the Looney Tunes can talk. The Road Runner doesn't talk."

"Hey, you're right," Willy said. "And that frog only sings when no one's looking."

"Yeah. And have you ever wondered how Marvin the Martian can know English if he's from another planet?" Bentley asked.

I listened to the hum of their voices as I looked over at the trees surrounding the reservoir. I thought about the UFO sightings and my weird nightmare.

Could there really be something out there? What would I do if I came face-to-face with an alien? How would we communicate?

Willy's voice interrupted my thoughts. "Look! It's that reporter. He's filming us."

I followed his gaze to a large white van parked along the nearby road. Sure enough, there was Treadweather. He stood there scribbling down notes on a legal pad and pointing out stuff for the cameraman to tape. Only it didn't seem as if he was just getting footage of the building for his report. Instead, Treadweather was studying the school yard, checking out each student and recording information.

What is he up to?

Just then, Treadweather glared in our direction. My mind shifted into defense mode. There *was* something about his eyes. I'd seen that cold, predatory stare before. It was the same look I saw on my dad's face whenever he went hunting.

"Look out!" someone yelled behind me.

I turned and saw the racquetball careening

wildly down the sidewalk. It bounced a few times, skittered off the pavement, and came rolling to a stop at my feet.

I picked it up and started to toss it back.

"Hey, it's the Karate Kid!" someone shouted. "Better watch your heads!"

"Yeah, he could probably ram it down someone's throat," another guy said.

Gary, Bentley, and Willy started chanting "E-than! E-than!"

I looked at the faces around me, all expectant and excited, waiting for me to launch the ball like a rocket. Then I felt Treadweather's icy stare.

Mr. Koto's warning flashed through my mind: *You are in danger. Do not draw attention to yourself.*

"E-than! E-than! E-than!" my buddies chanted.

Be like the snake. Remain still, hidden, cautious.

"Come on, Mighty Boy! Give us your best knuckleball!"

Sometimes the best weapon . . . is restraint.

As I stood there ready to throw, I suddenly realized something. I didn't want to be a superhero. There was a reason why Batman wore a mask. There was a reason why Clark Kent didn't live as Superman twenty-four hours a day. With villains constantly chasing you and people begging you for help all the time, you just had to protect yourself sometimes.

I reached back my arm and chucked the ball

toward the Whip-It game. It spun off my hand awkwardly, sailed wide, and stopped way short of its target.

All the kids who were watching shook their heads and walked off. My buddies were silent. Treadweather and his cameraman began loading up their van.

And I went back to being just Ethan.

_____ Chapter 11

I had to stay a little late after school so Principal Lower could give me my certificate of recognition for uncommon valor. It was a cheap, laser-printed doily with a shiny gold sticker at the bottom. Still, he handed it to me as if it were a Nobel peace prize.

I thanked him and said I'd treasure it always. Then, in the hallway, I folded it up and stuck it in my pants pocket.

After that, I had to talk to Coach Williams in the athletics office. Billy Harrison had quit the wrestling team and Coach wanted me to take his place. I guess he hadn't heard that I'd gone back to being a wimp.

I turned him down. I'd had enough fighting lately. Besides, I didn't want to risk calling attention to myself again.

When I walked back to my locker, it was open. Someone had managed to yank off the old, rusty lock and get inside.

Why would somebody do this? It's not like I have anything valu—

My heart began beating violently, threatening to break my ribs from the inside.

My comic book!

On the floor in front of me lay the ripped remains of the padded envelope. I looked down the hallway and saw a trail of wadded-up tissue paper.

I choked back the bitter taste in my mouth.

The path led through the locker area and hooked a right toward the gym. As I rounded the corner, the tissue paper wads ended. For a few yards there was nothing and then—

"No!"

Crumpled pages of the first edition littered the floor. There was Cyclops shredded and mangled. Ice Man's mutilated form was a few feet away.

Rage seeped through my body like hot glue, cementing my jaw shut and hardening my hands into tight fists.

I'm going to make them pay for this! I'll pound them! I'll hang them by their own tongues! They messed with the wrong guy!

I followed the line of fallen X-Men to the gym, my anger rising every step of the way. By the time I yanked open the heavy steel doors, I could practically feel the hatred in my veins.

It was dark and empty inside. The paper wads had stopped, but the thief was nowhere in sight.

"All right! Where are you?" I yelled. My words bounced off the walls like basketballs. "Come on out and face me!"

"Is this what you're looking for?" The voice was mocking and familiar.

Drew Molinari stepped into the dim light shining from under the doors. His face was twisted in a smirk. He was holding the empty comic-book cover.

"Give me that!" I growled.

"You know, someone really ought to talk to the janitor about all this trash," he said smugly. Then he started ripping the cover into tiny shreds.

My rage boiled over.

I jumped on Drew and started pummeling him. I felt as though months and months of pent-up fury finally erupted inside me.

Drew had no chance. Even with his massive legs and strong forearms, he was no match for me now. I knocked him back against the gym wall with a kick to his chest and doubled him over with a sharp punch in the stomach.

I should have stopped there, but I didn't. I couldn't.

I was too angry. I was out of control.

"Stop! Please!" he whimpered, shielding his face with his arms.

I didn't listen. I'm ashamed to admit it, but that

creature who lived inside of me wanted to see Drew suffer, and I couldn't seem to stop it.

My hands clamped around his throat almost as if they had a mind of their own.

Drew made a strange gurgling sound and tried to push me away.

I gripped tighter.

His skin turned purple.

I gripped tighter. Only I didn't want to anymore.

His arms went slack and his eyes met mine.

I wanted to let go. I knew it had gone way too far. But I couldn't stop.

"Go ahead, kill him . . . it's in your blood."

The cold, inhuman voice broke my trance.

I jumped away from Drew as if he was about to strangle me, not the other way around.

"Kill him?" I asked shakily, looking into the shadows.

Sometimes the best weapon . . . is restraint, came Mr. Koto's voice from inside me.

I stared down at Drew's unconscious form.

"Go ahead! Kill him!" It was that voice again. Terrifyingly creepy, but at the same time . . . familiar.

I looked up to see Martin Treadweather stepping from behind the bleachers.

Only it wasn't Treadweather at all. The thing had Treadweather's body and hairdo, but its eyes were two jet black disks.

"Did you think you could fool me," he asked, "simply by avoiding my questions? By pretending you couldn't throw a ball?"

I stood up straight and faced him. My knees were shaking.

"You were foolish to reveal yourself," he continued. "You brought me right to you."

As he spoke, he walked toward me. I wasn't going to let him distract me. I knew what he wanted.

My normal patterns of thought vanished and my instincts whirred into overdrive. I was sizing him up, estimating his strength and speed. I was the tiger, crouched and watchful. The falcon, circling and waiting.

"We will see if you possess your father's power," he said ominously. Then he sprang at me.

I was ready.

He flew toward me, but I ducked. I pushed him, using his own momentum against him. Treadweather crashed to the ground. Then, like some kind of psycho Weebil, he rolled right back to his feet.

He jumped at me again—only this time he dove lower, slamming into my stomach and knocking me flat.

I hunched over, unable to breathe. It felt as if my organs had been jolted out of their regular spots.

Those awful eyes loomed over me, shocking me out of my agony. I quickly rolled out of his path and scrambled to my feet.

Treadweather pivoted around and met me head-on.

The battle sped up. He started punching and kicking and pouncing so fast I couldn't separate the moves. I blocked and dodged, waiting for my chance to strike back when I sensed a weakness.

But I didn't. The guy made Kenji seem like a sixth-grade hall monitor. I was no match for him. Treadweather had perfect moves, the power of a hand grenade, and he didn't get tired. If this were *Mortal Kombat*, his energy bar would be at full power. Mine would be the width of a needle.

A sick feeling spread through my stomach as I found myself getting cornered inch by inch. My dodges and blocks were getting sloppier. His hand-to-hand fighting was getting stronger and faster.

I had to get away.

Believe it or not, Drew Molinari gave me my chance.

"Uuunnnhhh," Drew moaned from where he was lying across the room.

Treadweather stopped and took a step toward the noise.

That's when I ducked under his arm, slammed him hard against the wall with my shoulder, and ran.

As I broke free, I could feel Treadweather reach out for me. But his fingers only grazed the back of my shirt.

I raced through the gym and into the boys' locker

room. I shoved a heavy steel bench against the door, barricading it.

I knew it wouldn't keep him out. I just needed to buy some time.

The only other way out of the locker room was through a door on the opposite end. It opened into a tunnel that led to the football field, so that players could make a big entrance at the start of a game.

If I could make it outside, I was home free. Or at least I could get some help.

Bam!

The locker room door banged against the steel bench. Treadweather was out there. Luckily, the bench held. I ran past the lockers and burst through the rear exit.

The tunnel was creepy. It was long and narrow and dimly lit by bare, dangling lightbulbs. My footsteps gave off an eerie echo as I sprinted through the cavernous hallway, dodging sports gear and field equipment.

Finally I made it to the door at the far end. I pushed against it.

But the door wouldn't budge.

No matter how hard I slammed myself against the door, it stayed shut—locked from the outside. A total dead end.

Desperate, I ran back through the tunnel. I had to find some other way out. But just when I reached the door to the locker room, I heard the soul-jarring sound of a big metal bench being wrenched from its spot.

Treadweather had broken through my barricade. I was trapped.

I slunk against the wall of the tunnel, wondering what I could do. I knew I had only a few seconds before Treadweather found me. I had no weapons, hardly any strength left, and no one to guide me.

Feel the animal within you, Mr. Koto's voice sounded in my head.

Yeah. Right. Thanks a lot.

Be like the snake.

Wait a minute. That was it!

Quickly, I raced back through the tunnel, grabbed a stray badminton racket, and started smashing all the lightbulbs. Soon, the passageway was completely dark.

I felt my way over to a tackling dummy near the football field exit, crouched behind it, and waited.

It wasn't long before I saw Treadweather's dark silhouette in the doorway. Then the door slammed shut again. Everything went pitch black.

I sat in the darkness, listening to Treadweather's echoing steps.

I tried frantically to call up my thermal vision. I scrunched my eyes shut, pressed against the sockets, and begged whatever weird creature it was who lived inside me to please wake up *now*.

I lifted my eyelids. I was as blind as before.

Treadweather's footsteps grew louder. They were closing in. I could hear his raspy breath and smell his sickening cologne, but I couldn't see a thing.

"I feel your presence, Henley's son," he called out. "Why put off the inevitable? This world was never meant for you."

What was that supposed to mean? Without warning, my heat-sensing vision activated itself.

I peered out from behind the tackling dummy and saw Treadweather coming toward me, lighting up the tunnel like a bug-eyed ghost.

I waited until he was right in front of me. Then I shoved the tackling dummy into him as hard as I could, catching him off guard and knocking him backward. As he struggled to get up, I grabbed a soccer net off the floor and threw it over him.

I raced back through the tunnel and reached the door to the locker room. But when I tried to open it, it barely budged. Treadweather had tied it shut with a jump rope.

Luckily, my own hands glowed enough to show me where the knots were. While I worked urgently to unravel them, my superperipheral vision caught movement behind me.

I had less than a second to untie the rope. Somehow I did it, with my hands shaking, my eyes bugging, my muscles aching, and my teeth tingling.

But as soon as I threw myself against the door, Treadweather gripped my shoulder from behind.

I'm not sure what happened then. My intense fear and exhaustion turned those few seconds into a blur.

But I do know this much: I bit Treadweather's hand. Hard.

I remember him shouting in pain and releasing his grip.

I remember my teeth burning.

In a flash, I ducked away and burst into the locker room. My eyes squinted against the new light, but I still made my way. I raced past the lockers, hurdled the overturned bench, and threw open the gymnasium door.

I could hear Treadweather following fast, and I strained for whatever extra speed my legs could manage.

Before I could reach the exit, he tackled me.

"You cannot escape," he said, breathing heavy.

He knelt on my chest, pinning me down. For some reason, his palms felt like ice but his body was covered with sweat.

Then he started to morph. I'm not kidding.

His skin stretched and moved like Silly Putty, rearranging his face until it wasn't Treadweather any longer, but a different man—a man with sharp features and chalky skin. Only the coal black eyes remained the same.

"Son of Henley, one of the greatest warriors in the

galaxy," he said. "I knew you'd put up a good fight. Not like the Aldridge boy. He was such easy prey—hardly better than a human—whereas you . . . you were quite a slippery little sn—"

I didn't try to understand what he was saying. I just lay there waiting to die.

Then suddenly, he started convulsing.

His fingers let go of my throat.

I rolled away from him.

I watched in disbelief as his face contorted and he fell forward. His feet twitched, then he lay still.

I rolled him over and stared into his eyes. The blackness slowly constricted until they looked normal again—normal, but very dead.

"Metier Police Department."

I stood at the pay phone in front of the school building trembling. I tried to keep my voice steady as I asked to speak to my dad. A moment later, I heard his voice.

"Dad, it's Ethan."

"Ethan! Where have you been, son? Your mother was worried."

"Um, I think you ought to come up to the school, Dad."

"What's going on? Do you need a ride?"

"Yeah. But bring an ambulance, too."

Chapter 12

Dr. Strickrichter said I probably held the record for quickest return to the emergency room. But at least I wasn't hurt.

Drew, on the other hand, looked as if he came out of a juicer. I felt awful as I sat in a chair alongside Drew's hospital bed listening to my dad and some other investigators ask lots of questions—things such as: "How do you and Ethan know each other?" and "What were you doing in the gym after school?"

Mainly, though, they wanted to know about the dead guy.

Nobody knew who he was. He had no identification on him, and his fingerprints weren't on record. No one remembered seeing him enter the building. The investigators assumed he was the guy who abducted Todd Aldridge, that he was coming back to the school to get another victim.

"Did he say who he was or what he wanted?" one of the detectives asked.

"No," I answered.

"Did he give you any information about Todd? Where he might be? Whether he is alive?" another one asked.

"No," I answered, even though it wasn't completely true.

"How were you able to escape from him?" my dad asked.

"I ran and hid," I answered half truthfully, figuring I had better keep a low profile. It was for my own protection. I'd already had one superweirdo trying his best to kill me. From now on, I was taking Mr. Koto's advice. I would stay out of the limelight.

"What about you, Drew?" Dad asked, turning toward the bed.

Drew couldn't give them any answers, either. He said he couldn't remember anything that happened after school, not even the comic book or our fight in the gym. "I don't know. It's all fuzzy," he said over and over in a dopey voice.

I felt terrible that I'd beaten him up so bad. At least he was still alive. A few more seconds and I . . . I didn't even want to think about what could've happened.

With that in mind, I was glad Treadweather, or the Treadweather Thing, showed up.

The cops assumed that the stranger beat up Drew,

and even though I felt weird about it, I didn't tell them the truth. Besides, I doubt they would have accepted my version, anyway.

"And you say you have no idea what killed this guy?" one of the detectives asked me for the fifth time.

"No."

"Well," he said with a sigh. "If you fellas remember anything at all that might help us out, give us a call." The investigators shook my dad's hand, nodded at Drew and me, and left.

"Son, we need to let Drew get his rest," my dad said.

"Okay." I stood up and followed him to the door.

"Bye," Drew said groggily. "See you at school." You'd think we were best friends.

Dad and I walked down the hallway to the waiting room.

"I need to go sign some forms and call your mother. You know, she's been worried sick about you these past few days. We both have." My dad cracked his knuckles uncomfortably.

"I know," I responded, looking right into his eyes. "But you don't need to worry anymore. It's all over with now."

Dad knitted up his brow and studied me for a moment, considering the true meaning behind my words.

"I mean it, Dad. I'm going to be fine. I can take care of myself," I added.

"I'm starting to think you can, son," he said. Then he punched my arm and walked over to the front desk.

I may not have his blood in my veins, but I was beginning to understand my dad.

He was like a comic book. If you read him right, you could get a lot out of him.

After waiting around a few minutes, I decided I was hungry and walked over to a nearby vending machine. As I stood there trying to decide between red licorice or a chocolate bar, a manicured hand suddenly clamped on my shoulder.

I turned around to see Martin Treadweather grinning fiendishly at me.

"Aaauuugh!" I shouted at the top of my lungs. I'm surprised my hair didn't turn completely white.

"Hey, kid. Martin Treadweather, Channel Three News. I understand you had a pretty interesting evening. Care to give an interview?"

I stared into his eyeballs, but saw nothing behind them. Really. Nothing at all. He seemed about as threatening as a toaster oven.

"No comment," I muttered.

Treadweather gave a fake chuckle. "You're a pretty spunky kid. Guess I should know better than to mess with you, huh?" He crouched down like a boxer and threw a couple of weak air punches in my direction. "But seriously, how about you tell all the concerned Metierites about your recent adventure?"

I was seriously tempted to throw him into the candy machine and gag him with a cup cake, but I was practicing restraint from now on.

I opened my mouth, about to point him in the direction of a nearby cliff, when someone grabbed him from behind.

My father stood holding Treadweather by his Armani shirt collar.

"All right, buddy. Take your news crew, your microphone, and your giant teeth, and get out before I cite you for obstruction of police business."

"Oh? What business?" Treadweather asked suspiciously.

Dad pointed at me. "He's my son. He's my business."

Treadweather backed out sheepishly, just as Dr. Strickrichter entered the waiting room.

"Chief Rogers, I need to talk to you for a moment," she said. She looked pale and a little spooked. "We just got the lab work back on the deceased suspect. We know what killed him. We just don't know how."

"What did you find?" Dad asked.

"The preliminary autopsy shows that the stranger died of a massive dose of neurotoxins—proteinase, adenosine triphosphatase, phosphodiesterase . . ."

"What does that mean exactly?" my dad interrupted.

Dr. Strickrichter looked from my dad to me and back to my dad. "We think he was bitten by a snake. A snake more venomous than any species on record."

* * *

119

I don't know how long I stood there in that waiting room. I didn't notice the doctor leaving. I noticed my dad trying to talk to me, but I didn't hear what he said.

A snake. A venomous snake.

It couldn't be. They did the tests wrong, I told myself. It was some kind of weird, flukey mistake.

So why couldn't I get rid of the image of my teeth chomping down on the Treadweather Thing's hand?

I shook my head, yanking myself back to reality. I had to forget it. I had to forget about all the psycho things that had happened to me in the last few days. *From now on, I'll be ordinary Ethan. The one without special powers. The one no one notices.*

"Hi, Ethan!" a girl's voice called.

Yvonne walked past us, flashing me a gorgeous smile.

Well . . . I guess it'd be all right if a few people notice.

"Come on, son. It's late," my dad said, patting me on the back. "Your mom has dinner waiting."

We left the hospital and walked through the parking lot to the squad car. It was dark out and the stars were sparkling overhead.

The ride home was quiet, but it wasn't the uncomfortable silence we usually had. It was more relaxed. This time no one needed to say anything.

Still, I couldn't help wondering about my real father. Who was Henley? Who—or what—was the

Treadweather Thing? And why did he want to kill me? Now that Mr. Koto was dead, who could I ask?

The police radio crackled.

"Bzzzt! Bzzzt! Calling car fourteen."

"Fourteen, here. Over."

"Chief Rogers, we have more reports of strange lights in the sky over the reservoir."

"Not again," Dad moaned.

I looked through the window and cast my eyes to the night sky.

This world was never meant for you. That's what the Treadweather creature had said.

As scary as it was to admit it to myself, deep down I knew that was true. I was different. Maybe I had known it for a long time.

Funny. People always think of aliens as coming from outer space.

I found one under my own skin.

Turn the page for a
special sneak peek of

Alien Blood

Available From
MINSTREL Paperbacks

_____ Alien Blood

"I wouldn't normally bother you with this till you were a hundred percent, but it's important to get this information while it's still fresh in your head," the chief said.

He, my dad, and I were up in my room. My dad was sitting on the edge of the bed, I was in it, and the chief was sitting across from me in my desk chair. He was a big man—the chair was way too little for him. He held a clipboard balanced on his knees.

"I want you to think of anything you can that can help us track this man down, Ashley." Chief Rogers leaned forward. The chair creaked. "Any detail at all, no matter how small."

I told him everything that had happened to me the night before, starting at swim practice and ending at the reservoir. I concentrated hard on telling him everything I'd seen of the man who'd been chasing me.

Which amounted to basically nothing.

I couldn't tell him how old the man was. I hadn't seen what he was wearing. I didn't get a good enough look to guess his height or weight.

When I was finished, the chief frowned.

"That doesn't give us a lot to go on, Ashley." He thought a moment. "At the hospital, you said something about his eyes."

"Yeah." I hesitated. The memory of the man's eyes—or the black disks where his eyes should have been—was just as vivid in my mind as it had been the night before. Only sitting here, in the cold light of day, it seemed impossible that I'd actually seen what I was remembering now.

"Maybe I was hallucinating," I said. "But I could have sworn that he . . ." My voice trailed off. I shook my head. "Here."

I grabbed my notebook off the night table and ripped a page out. When I finished drawing, I held up the page for the chief. "This is what his eyes looked like."

"Like a bug's eyes," the chief said.

"Exactly!" I said. I smiled at the chief.

He was looking at my father, shaking his head.

He doesn't believe me.

"Maybe there's some kind of medical condition that makes your eyes look like that," my dad offered.

"Maybe. It's something we can check on," the chief said. He picked up the drawing and stood. "Mind if I take this?"

"Not at all," I said. "If you think it'll help."

"Feel better, Ashley," he said.

And then he was gone.

At three o'clock, I had another visitor.

"Oh, Ashley!"

Jenny ran across the room and gave me a big hug.

"Youch!" I flinched. She'd managed to squeeze me where I was sorest.

"Sorry," Jenny said, stepping away. Her eyes were glistening. "This is terrible," she said. "*Look* at you."

"Gee, thanks, Jen. Nice to see you, too."

"You know what I mean. I can't believe what happened."

"I can't, either." I didn't know what else to say.

"Have the police caught him? The man who was chasing you?" Jenny asked.

"How did you hear about that?" I asked.

Jenny shrugged. "It's all over school."

"Oh, that's great." The thought of being talked about by everyone in school didn't appeal to me.

"But you're feeling all right?" Jenny asked.

I paused a moment.

I always told Jenny everything. When I stole a pack of gum from the drugstore on a dare, I told her. When I lied about leaving my math homework at home, I told her. When I thought I'd had a crush on Jack Raynes—that airhead—I told her.

One night, when I was at a sleep-over at her house, I'd even told her how jealous I was of her, because she has a mother.

But telling her what had just happened to me— that, I didn't think I could do. Especially after the look Chief Rogers gave me when I showed him my picture of the man's eyes.

I didn't want everyone in the world to think I was crazy.

"Yeah," I said. "Feeling fine."

Jenny frowned. She didn't look as though she believed me.

I noticed she was hiding something behind her back, so I decided to change the subject.

"What's that?"

"Oh—this?" She held up a tiny velvet box with a little bow wrapped around it. "It's a little something for you." She handed it to me. "A day late, but the sentiment is genuine."

"Hey, thanks," I said. I took the box from her and untied the ribbon.

Inside were a pair of silver earrings. They were shaped like tiny masks—one happy, one sad.

"They're drama masks," Jenny explained. "Comedy and tragedy. I know how much you love movies, and . . . well, they're *kind* of related."

"Thanks, Jen. They're perfect." I lifted out the "comedy" mask and raised it to my ear. "I think for now I'll just wear this one. I've had enough tragedy to last me until I'm at least—"

I was having trouble getting my new earring in. I couldn't find the hole in my earlobe. After a couple more failed jabs, I set the box down and tried again using both hands.

It still wouldn't go in.

"Here, let me do that." Jenny sat down next to me, taking the earring in one hand and my earlobe in the other. She frowned. Then she turned my head and looked at my other ear. Her frown deepened. "Uh . . . Ash?"

"What is it?" I asked.

"Your ears *are* pierced, aren't they?"

"Jen," I said, looking her in the eye. "You know they are."

"Well, I don't know how to tell you this, Ashley. But they're not anymore."

"What? What are you talking about?"

I got up out of bed and crossed to my dresser. I bent over and peered at my ears in the mirror. First at one earlobe, then the other.

Jenny was right. There was no trace of a hole in either ear.

A huge lump formed in my throat. I swallowed it down hard.

"How—how can that be?" I asked.

Jenny must have detected the panic in my voice.

"Hey," she said, coming up beside me. She put a hand on my shoulder. "I'm sure there's some logical explanation."

She led me back to my bed. I climbed in.

"Besides," she added, fluffing my pillow and tucking it under my head, "you can always get them pierced again."

I nodded. "I guess so. . . ."

Jenny smiled at me reassuringly.

"How 'bout this? As soon as you're feeling up to it, we'll go to the mall, catch that movie you wanted to see, and get your ears pierced—I mean, repierced. Whatever. How does that sound?"

I smiled weakly. "It sounds like a plan."

"Good." Jenny jumped up off my bed and headed for the door. On her way out, she turned. "And we can get your nails done, too," she said. She blew me a kiss and left.

Get my nails done? What was she talking about?

I looked down at my fingers.

The nail polish on my right hand was completely gone, but the polish on my left hand was still there.

A new lump formed in my throat. *What's going on here?*

Had the polish come off when I fell through the

ice? Did the cold water somehow make it dissolve? If so, why had it only come off *one* hand?

More likely someone had removed it in the emergency room. It was probably some kind of weird hospital procedure—like when my dad had his heart operation and they shaved his entire chest.

But why would they remove my nail polish? It seemed ridiculous.

And why were my ears no longer pierced? *That* seemed downright impossible.

I sighed, rolled over, and buried my face in my pillow. It was all too much to think about.

Being chased by that man with the freaky eyes. Falling through the ice and nearly drowning. Now this new stuff with my ears and nails.

What other surprises were in store for me?

If I had known the answer to that question, I would have stayed in my bed for the rest of my life.

But the next morning, to my surprise (and my dad's), I felt well enough to go to school.

"You shouldn't rush things," he told me over breakfast. "Are you sure you don't want to take a couple days to rest up?"

I shook my head and pulled a Pop-Tart out of the box on the table.

"No," I said. "I'm fine, Dad, honest." And I really was—I couldn't believe how much better I'd felt waking up this morning. The nasty bruise was still there, but the pain in my chest had completely gone away. I felt like myself again.

Well, make that a starving version of myself.

I was on my second Pop-Tart. And I'd already had two bowls of cereal. I ate so much, in fact, that we got a late start leaving. I got to school just in time for homeroom.

Mrs. Martinez, my homeroom teacher, was sitting at her desk grading some papers when I walked in. When she saw me, her eyebrows shot up.

"Ashley," she said. "I didn't expect to see *you* today."

Mrs. Martinez was known as the strictest teacher at Metier Junior High. In fact, the only time I've ever gotten detention was for being late to homeroom.

So I nearly choked when Mrs. Martinez suddenly *smiled* at me.

"How are you feeling?" she asked. She even sounded concerned.

"Much better, thank you," I said.

I walked to the back row of the class. Jenny was sitting in her seat already, doodling in her notebook. She hadn't seen me come in.

I cleared my throat.

"Good morning," I said.

Jenny looked up. Her eyes bugged out.

"*Ash?* Get out of town! What are you doing here?"

"Hey, I work here," I said, sitting down.

"Yeah, I guess you do." She tilted her head and examined me. "You look so much . . . *better*."

"I *feel* so much better."

It was true. Maybe it was owing to the giant breakfast I had eaten, but whatever the reason, I felt totally energized.

If people were expecting to see some shriveled, pale accident victim, then they were going to be disappointed. Hopefully, seeing me now, they wouldn't even give me a second glance.

Which was exactly how I wanted it.

I opened my backpack and took out my notebook, just as the PA speaker at the front of the classroom crackled to life.

"Brace yourself," Jenny said, leaning over. I rolled my eyes.

Every four weeks, Metier Junior High elected a new "student of the month." The winner got his or her name engraved on a bronze plaque that hung outside the lunchroom. The winner also got to lead the entire school in the flag salute each morning. Every school day for the past three weeks we'd been greeted by the congested sinuses of October's reigning SOTM, Ms. Debbi Schnur.

But not this morning.

"Good morning students. This is Principal Lower speaking."

"Hey, I guess we're being spared," Jenny muttered, removing her fingers from her ears.

I smiled at her and listened to the announcements. First with only one ear, and then with a growing sense of panic.

Because Mr. Lower was talking about *me*.

". . . to create a safe place here to educate you students, but unfortunately, the real world has a habit of cutting in on us," he was saying. "I want to remind you to be careful—especially going home after school. Especially after what happened a couple days ago."

So much for not getting a second glance.

As if on cue, the entire class turned around to stare at me.

I sank lower in my seat, hoping I could disappear.

"Don't be shy," Jenny whispered. "This is your fifteen minutes of fame."

I glared at her.

Mr. Lower kept talking. "We've arranged with the police department to have an officer and a patrol car around school. If you see anyone—or anything—suspicious in the vicinity, please report them immediately. Thank you."

The PA crackled again and went silent.

The other kids continued to stare at me like I'd done something wrong. Like it was all my fault some psycho had been after me.

Things just keep getting worse and worse, I thought to myself. *What next?*

In response, Debbi Schnur's nasal whine pierced through the loudspeaker:

"Good bording, Betierites! Please rise for the salute to the flag!"

*   *   *

My first-period class was English, with Mr. Blanchard.

Mr. Blanchard had longish blond hair and a beard. He looked sort of like Brad Pitt—only smarter. A lot of the girls in my grade had crushes on him, which I thought was kind of immature.

This morning, when I entered his classroom, Mr. Blanchard was writing something on the blackboard. Seeing me, he set down his chalk and fixed me with his big, hazel eyes.

"Ashley. How are you feeling?"

"Much better, thanks." Though I'd given the same answer at least a hundred times that morning, this time I felt my face turning red.

Maybe it's not all bad, being the center of attention.

I took my seat, cheeks burning, just as the late bell rang.

"All right, class."

Mr. Blanchard walked around to the front of his desk, then perched on the edge of it. "Let's pick up where we left off last class. We were talking about *Wuthering Heights*, about how each generation seemed doomed to repeat the mistakes of the previous one."

Wuthering Heights? I thought. The class must have just started that book yesterday.

Great. I miss one lousy day of school and already I'm behind.

I opened my notebook and flipped to the English section, to the last day I'd taken notes—Tuesday.

A chill ran down my spine.

The notes were all about *Wuthering Heights*.

I flipped back a day.

Monday's notes were on *Wuthering Heights*, too.

I paged back in my notebook frantically. My hands were shaking.

We'd been talking about the book for over a week. How could I have forgotten it?

I bent down, reaching for my backpack, and caught Becky Hanratty staring at me. Becky had the seat to my left.

I reached into my backpack and pulled out a handful of books.

One of them was *Wuthering Heights*.

My name was written in the inside cover. In my handwriting.

I flipped through the book. There were handwritten notes in the margins, all throughout.

I'd read this entire book.

But I couldn't remember any of it.

I raised my hand. "Mr. Blanchard?" My voice sounded faint and far away to me.

"Yes, Ashley?" He'd been in the middle of saying something. I'd interrupted him.

"Ashley?" he repeated. He was waiting for me to continue.

I couldn't get the words out.

"Is everything all right?"

I cleared my throat. "May I be excused? I'm not feeling well."

Concern flashed across his face. "Of course," he said. "Do you want to go to the nurse's—"

I got up and hurried past him. "No, no," I said. "I'll be fine. I'll be fine."

I felt twenty pairs of eyes staring at my back as I ran from the room.

I ran down the hall into the girls' room, ducked into one of the stalls, and sat there.

I'd forgotten reading a whole book.

Forgotten ever writing notes on it.

What was the matter with me?

I must have sat there in the bathroom for ten minutes. Not thinking. Not moving. Just staring into space. Just listening to the faucet.

Drip . . . drip . . . drip . . .

I shivered. Tears welled up in my eyes.

In movies, people lost their memories all the time. They got shot, or fell, or were hit in the head, and the next thing you knew they were going, "Who am I?" and forgetting who their wives were, or where they'd spent their childhood, or that they'd been an assassin for the U.S. government.

But this wasn't like the movies. I *knew* who *I* was.

The only thing I'd forgotten (as far as I could tell) was reading *Wuthering Heights.*

So what had happened to me?

Was it like amnesia in the movies, where you just need to get knocked in the head again and your memory comes back? Or was I going to keep forgetting things for the rest of my life? Or finding out new things I'd forgotten? And then forgetting that I'd forgotten that I'd—

Stop it, Ash.

I sighed. This wasn't getting me anywhere.

I got up and splashed my face with cold water. Then I headed back to English class, my mind still in a whir.

On the bright side, I reasoned, at least amnesia gave me a cool excuse for not having my homework done.

On the other hand, maybe this amnesia was a symptom of something worse. Brain damage, or something.

Wasn't *that* a pleasant thought.

Mr. Dailey, the janitor, was standing in the hall just down from the classroom door, working on one of the lockers. As I approached, he stopped his tinkering and stared at me.

I was getting sick of being stared at.

If he asks me how I'm feeling, I'll just scream.

I nodded at him and started to enter the classroom—

"Ashley," Mr. Dailey said.

I stopped, turned, and braced myself for the question of the day.

Something about Mr. Dailey looked different. The way he was standing, the way he was looking at me . . .

His eyes were flat black disks.

I froze.

He took a step toward me.

"Oh, my god." I couldn't breathe. I couldn't move. "You—"

"Don't be frightened," he said, lowering his voice. "I just wanted to ask you—"

The door to the classroom opened and Becky Hanratty stepped out, right in between us. She didn't see Mr Dailey.

"Oh, Ashley," she said. "Mr. Blanchard just sent me to check on how you—"

"Becky," I managed to choke out.

She frowned. "Ashley, are you all right? You look pale."

"Me? Am *I* all right?" I pointed at Mr. Dailey. Becky spun to face him. "Why don't you ask *him* how—"

His eyes were back to normal.

"Ashley?" Becky said.

I dropped my hand. "But . . ."

Mr. Dailey came toward me. He reached out and put his hand on my shoulder. It took every ounce of self-control I had not to scream.

"Is something the matter?" Mr. Dailey asked. "Should we take you to the infirmary?"

I stepped back, twisting out of his reach. "No. I'm fine. Let's go, Becky."

I pushed the classroom door open and stepped inside. Becky and Mr. Dailey stared after me like I was crazy.

Maybe I was.